I0642675

IM PRESS

ILYA EHRENBURG

The D.E. TRUST

A History of Europe's Destruction

BOSTON · 2025

ILYA EHRENBURG
The D.E. Trust. *A History of Europe's Destruction*

Translated into English by Alexander Pinsky

ISBN 978-1960533784

Published by M·GRAPHICS | BOSTON, MA
   ✉ mgraphics.books@gmail.com
   💻 mgraphics-books.com

Book Design by Yulia Timoshenko © 2025
Cover Design by Larysa Studinskaya © 2025

Printed in the U.S.A.

Contents

Translator's note

This book was written as a warning. That warning went largely unheeded at the time of its publication in Russian and in a few foreign translations (German, Czech and Japanese) that were published shortly afterwards. My aim as its translator was to make that warning heeded by the English-speaking audience because it is as relevant today as it was in 1923 — the year it was first published. In fact, some pages of this book read as if they were just written today, not over a century ago. This book is a dystopia, and as a matter of fact, one of the first dystopias ever written. It is also a bitter satire, and as most books of this genre may be found offensive and disturbing by many readers. It is certainly not the most pleasant reading, not the stuff for faint-hearted. It just shows the reader that a fatal mixture of greed, hubris and folly is more likely to destroy the most advanced civilization than any natural cataclysm.

No wonder then that this book was written by the eyewitness of the greatest man-made catastrophes of XX century: both world wars, Russian revolution and the Holocaust. Ilya Ehrenburg (1891–1967) was born in Kiev and grew up in Moscow. He attended prestigious school in Moscow. He got involved in the revolutionary activities at the time of the first Russian revolution of 1905–07, was arrested and expelled from school and was forced to emigrate at the age of 16. He spent most of his years in exile in France where he met and befriended Pablo Picasso, Diego Rivera, Amedeo Modigliani and other great artists and literary figures, served as a war correspondent with French army in WWI, returned to Russia at the time of the revolution of 1917 only to leave it again in 1921 after being disillusioned and repelled by the atrocities of Russian civil war. These feelings found their reflection in his poem "Prayer for Russia" (1918) and in his first novel "Julio Jurenito" (1922). He spent most of 1920–30s travelling across Europe and briefly visiting Soviet Russia. He served as a war correspondent for Soviet newspapers during the Civil war in Spain. He returned to Soviet Union in 1940 after the fall of France in WWII.

In 1941–45 he was one of the leading war correspondents of Red Army. After the war he was a prominent anti-war activist. He published his three-volume memoir "People, Years, Life" in 1960s where he revived many names that were thought to be erased forever from the memory of most Russians at the time of Stalin's purges. He died in Moscow in 1967.

1

Mr. Twyweight's early breakfast

On the eleventh of April, 1927 at 9:15 AM Mr. Twyweight, the owner of the largest meat packing company in Chicago had commenced his early breakfast.

Unlike most of his fellow Americans, who began their breakfasts with eggs, Mr. Twyweight always ate pears from California and yogurt first and then eggs as well. On that memorable morning, he as his custom dictated picked a large and juicy fruit and began to contemplate the profitability of buying the stock of his competitor's Mr. Cheers enterprise, meanwhile dripping the juice of the pear on a napkin. He wrote in his small notebook:

```
Pigs per hour — 820 per day 8200 per year  . . 2,492,800
Sheep " — 900(X10) 9000(X394) . . . . . . . . 2,736,000
Oxen " — 460 " 4600" . . . . . . . . . . . . . 1,398,400
Canned meat . . . . . . . . . . . . . . . . . . 31,000,000
Sausages . . . . . . . . . . . . . . . . . . . . 2,000,000
Blood (to Mr. Choate's sugar refinery) . . . . . . 700,000
Innards (for sausages, local util.) . . . . . . . . . . . —
Horns (to comb factory "Electra") . . . . . . . 1,200, 000
Other refuse (approx.) . . . . . . . . . . . . . 1,600,000
```

After that Mr. Twyweight uttered "Hmm" clearly expressing his doubts.

Still holding a pencil in his right hand, he ate a cup of yogurt and wrote on a special page of his notebook:

1. *Find out to whom exactly Cheers sells the stomachs and for how much.*

It is important to note that the first quarter of an hour of Mr. Twyweight's early breakfast was not completely devoted to the calculations of Mr. Cheers's profits and devouring of a Californian pear and yogurt. He also managed to make a brilliant discovery.

All scientists who worked on the biography of that outstanding organizer of the best meatpacking factory in the world came to the unanimous conclusion that with Mr. Twyweight's departure America lost a brilliant philosopher who had enriched the treasury of scientific thought with his numerous publications in the areas of zoo-psychology, anthroposophy, and eugenics. His name, which is now only familiar to a few specialists studying the history of Europe's demise in his time, i.e. in the mid-1920's through the late 1930's, was as popular in the USA as the name of the famous pen manufacturer Mr. Waterman and the heavy weight boxing champion Mr. Jampes. Three events were especially important for Mr. Twyweight's popularity:

1. He once has read in a newspaper that every man excretes per year:
Solid excrement . . . . .48.8 kg
Liquid refuse . . . . 438 kg
Costing $2.65
Which are wasted. And to promote rational economy he signed an agreement with one suburban kitchen garden enterprise where he travelled daily in his automobile at 9:30 AM right after eating his pear and eggs. This heroic deed of Mr. Twyweight was mentioned by the newspapers of every state, from Alaska to Mexican border.
2. In 1926 Mr. Twyweight had dictated to his female stenographer a short but very thoughtful essay on eugenics, while taking sulfuric bath: "Our moral duty, or on necessity of multiplying rationally". It was published in a small booklet with appropriate illustrations and turned

out to be great success. In the state of Ohio all the best graduates of elementary schools were awarded that booklet by Mr. Twyweight.

Even those who shunned reading books were still familiar with his name due to his vast and diverse activities. Should a random passerby, say in the 5th Avenue in NYC raise his eyes to the sky, he would immediately see a purple image of a young delicate pig enwreathed with the inscription:

JUST ASK FOR TWYWEIGHT'S FILET

So, great Mr. Twyweight having just finished eating his pear and calculating the profits of Cheers blessed the world with another discovery, namely, after recalling the highly acculturated entertainments of yesterday — watching a swimming competition and listening to the singing of famous soprano Mrs. Aide — he wrote in his notebook:

2 Prove beyond doubt that man originated from a frog (discovered by me — T.)

Despite the profundity of this thought it was not the reason April 11, 1927 may be truthfully named an historical date.

Events of utter importance happened later. The early breakfast of Mr. Twyweight went on.

A lackey brought a midsize egg in a silver cup. Mr. Twyweight carefully took off the shell on top of the egg and suddenly shuddered: in the colorless goo of egg white there was a small but distinct bloody spot. Mr. Twyweight pushed the egg away, visibly disturbed. The owner of a meatpacking factory where no less than eleven thousand pigs and seven hundred and eighty oxen were slaughtered daily was a vegetarian, and according to Lord's commandment was merciful to the beasts and sustained himself predominantly on fruit and dairy products. Once he spotted blood in egg white he fell into deep contemplation: does prevention of birth amount to murder, and if so, how can a devout vegetarian feed on eggs? After a minute hesitation he stirred the egg white with a spoon and then decidedly pushed it away and resolved not to eat eggs for breakfast, lunch, or dinner, unlike the rest of Americans.

But not even that touching decision made April 11, 1927 the day of glory. Removing an inedible egg the lackey gave Mr. Twyweight his morning mail, over thirty letters. Mr. Twyweight sorted out eleven envelopes with European stamps and threw them in the waste basket unread. He hated Europe that did not want to buy his canned meat and multiply in a rational way. Quickly scanning the rest of his mail, he fixed his attention on the last letter. The following was printed on a crispy sheet:

#32174

Trust Company for the Destruction of Europe
April 10, 1927
To: Mr. Twyweight in Chicago, Il

Dear Sir,
The present is to inform you that according to the resolution of the Trust Co. on April 4 this year we commence the realization of the discussed plan of the destruction of Europe.
My absolute regards,
Jens Boot, Director.

— Very well, — uttered Mr. Twyweight and took a note in his notebook.

After that he unfolded an issue of "Chicago Tribune." His eyes unwillingly stopped at the bottom of the fourth column, where the word "Europe" stood and now occupied his thoughts and deeds. He boringly dragged his eyesight over the number of cables that reported on the all kinds of wars in the Balkans and Rhine states. Only three reports were about peaceful business:

Geneva. Chairman of the League of Nations Mr. Bargos, at the banquet in honor of the tenth anniversary of that organization made a speech noting the brilliant successes of the policies of peace, humanism, and justice despite multiple complications. Representative of Luxembourg declined the invitation to the festivities. Lilac dress of M-me Traindadais, vice-president's spouse designed by M-r. LeBain (Paris, 2 Rue de la Paix) was of note. Menu: assorted appetizers, turtle soup, sole a la Grenadine, filet de la paix, asparagus with sauce Lamberon, ice cream Fjord.

Copenhagen, Institute of Higher Statistics

Reports that the loss of lives in 1924–26 exceeds the number of casualties in World war of 1914–18. As everyone knows the war cost in Europe were:

```
Killed in action. . . . . . . . . . . . . . . . .   10, 200,000
Decline in birth rate . . . . . . . . . . . . .   20, 850,000
Increase in mortality  . . . . . . . . . . . .   6,700,000
All . . . . . . . . . . . . . . . . . . . . . . . . . .37,750,000
```

```
In the years 1924–26.
Killed (in national and civil wars)  . . . . . . .  9,600,000
Decline in birth rate (compared to 1913) . .  18,000,000
Increase in mortality (malnutrition,
epidemics, etc.)  . . . . . . . . . . . . . . . . .  28,000,000
All . . . . . . . . . . . . . . . . . . . . . . . . . .  55,600,000
```

Venice: The false rumors of Gabriele D'Annunzio' s death are dispelled.

The great poet is alive and well and just finished a new ode "On the annexation of Macedonia."

He plans a weeklong trip to former Greece. The poet considers taking part in the sport events (motor sled riding on the slopes of Mt. Olympus). Dante's Memorial Society presented the poet on this occasion with green suede breeches and mittens designed in the shape of lyres.

After finishing the cables Mr. Twyweight looked at the wall where among other charts and diagrams was the big map of both hemispheres. Once the charming daughter of the Phoenician king and now a miserable whore, Europe was taking her regular bath. Mr. Twyweight poked it in the forehead, his index finger hitting Madrid. Done with his early breakfast he went to the kitchen garden company as usually. His notebook was left at his desk.

April 11, 1927, to do:

1. Find out to whom Cheers sell the stomachs and for how much.

2. Prove beyond doubt that man originated from a frog (discovered by me — T.)

3. Destroy Europe.

2

Other Events of that Memorable Day

That same morning the identical letters with the letterhead of D. E. Trust Co. and signature of Jens Boot were received by two other members of the company's board, Messrs. Jabbs and Hardyle.

Mr. Jabbs was also having his early breakfast consisting of eggs and ham (he wasn't a vegetarian).

Mr. Hardyle pushing away a tray with coffee drank only soda (he had more than his fair share of cocktails last night).

After reading the letters they quite approved the diligence of Jens Boot.

Mr. Jabbs even squinted with pleasure and chewed on a thick unlit cigar forgetting to light it up.

Mr. Hardyle used a letter to tickle a charming Javan girl that curled up at his feet.

Mr. Jabbs was in Pittsburgh, PA, and Mr. Hardyle — in Boston, MA.

They have finished their breakfast. A bath that Europe was taking at that time must be rather called the afternoon one. The dusty clock at Friedrichstrasse Station in Berlin was showing 5:58PM. Disheveled gray-haired woman that stood under the clock was yelling: "Be-uer!"

No one was buying newspapers that reported on the anniversary of the League of Nations, sixteen different wars and green breeches of Gabriele D'Annunzio. The woman's yell got weaker and weaker and then at last died out completely.

Then a neatly attired young man with orange gloves rushed to her side, snatched a newspaper out of her hands and gave her a small 100,000 marks bill. Poor woman could not take it because she passed away at 5:59 PM after showing remarkable resilience. But instead of showing respect to a lady that managed to die standing upright, the young man hastily unfolded the newspaper and froze over the stock exchange report:

	April 10	April 11
US Dollar	60,800,000	54,000,000
RF Franc	3,210,000	2,970,000
Thaler	89,000	81,000
Ruble	450	415

"Mein Gott!" — he moaned and sat on the pavement. His heavenly blue right eye covered with an eyeglass shed a stream of tears that spilled on a dusty sidewalk of dilapidated and half-ruined Berlin.

"Mein Gott!" — mumbled a doctor trying to feel nonexistent pulse of a dead paper peddler. — No carbohydrates, neither fat, nor protein — hundred and eighth case just today.

"Mein Gott!" — whispered the girlfriend of young man fraulein Mizzi. — It's black Wednesday. Ninety-four went bankrupt, six committed suicide and Otto broke his eyeglass.

Everything was as usual. Not just in Berlin, but in all of Europe nothing remarkable happened.

In Bergen (5:18 PM) fisherman Christens took his boots off and pulled ashore a slimy flounder. American lady aimed her Kodak at him and smiled. As a matter of fact, nobody bought his flounder.

In Paris (5:07 PM) banks were closing. M-r Violle exited the building of Credit Lyonnais, waved his cane, adjusted a handkerchief in his breast pocket and waited for a bus. His handkerchief was stolen while he was boarding a bus. M-r Violle cursed the government and lost his appetite.

In Genoa (5:47 PM) steamer "Caesar" docked. A whore named Pireta pointed to American sailor at her skirt and purse. The sailor got the hint and followed her around the nearest corner. Pireta dreaded malaria and wore a garland of garlic bulbs on her neck to ward off the pestilence. The sailor didn't like the smell of it and paid her nothing.

In Kozlov (7:42 PM) commissar Vanya Globov was interrogating a petty thief who stole a turtle shell lorgnette that belonged to the itinerant director of "Timber Trust." Globov was utterly bored. The thief begged pardon and his guard cursed and kicked his butt now and then with his government issue boot. Commissar's daughter was rehearsing revolutionary melodies behind the wall. Globov produced two photographs out of his breast pocket, one of Sonya Zaykina and one of Karl Marx. Sonya cheated on him. Marx passed away long time ago. Vanya yawned and stretched himself on a sofa.

So it was going in old decrepit Europe in that hour. Somebody was honored in Lisbon and someone was shot in Budapest. In those places where neither speeches, nor shots were heard one still could hear snoring, clocks' ticking, drunken hiccups and rumbling of hungry stomachs. The seas were roaring as usual, the southern ones with their octopi and colorful shells, the western ones with their lobsters that looked like self-important professors and the northern ones swarming with silver herring.

In the mountains where the heels of the Lazy One were resting a pillar stood as usual. According to the order of local authorities it was freshly painted and the inscription on it informed:

Europe ← . . . . → Asia
A sparrow roosted on the pillar.

Absolutely no one was thinking of the pillar, neither of the seas, nor of Europe's destiny.

Only far, far away in another hemisphere where the clock showed 9:30 AM where the workday morning was underway the director of secret "D. E. Trust Co." Jens Boot bent over the map of Europe and issued bold directives to eighteen thousand six hundred and seventy agents of the company located in all countries of Europe.

3
The Root of Evil, or Ethnographic Curiosity of the Prince of Monaco

The prince of Monaco, being the potentate of one of the tiniest states of Europe (area 1.5 square km, population 24,600 people) was, according to most historians, a man of immense curiosity. All his time free from the thorough studies of the game of roulette was devoted to travelling. Europe owes its demise to precisely these propensities of that thoughtful monarch.

In the spring of 1892, the prince travelled to Holland. He spent three days in the Hague and was utterly captivated, even broke in tears seeing the impossible beauty of the XVII century painting by Jan Maas that depicted a copper basin. In Gouda the prince purchased a pipe, in Haarlem — a tulip bulb, and in Leyden — a young prophet. Prince kept a diary that fortunately survived and showed us the colorful life in that part of Europe at the end of XIX century.

On June 18 the prince embarked on a small yacht at the northern town of Den Helder and at about 2:00PM landed on a low shore of the isle of Texel whose small population was mostly employed in collection of eggs of the sea birds, as was recently discovered by Mr. Bearway.

Passing by a small house the prince noticed a few red heads of Dutch cheese. His thought at the moment were occupied by his beloved roulette, that's why he threw one of the heads of cheese and shouted the words of croupier: "Make your bets!"

Nice looking young Dutchess with gentle soft facial expression wearing a starched oorijzer on her head came out, picked up the head of cheese that had rolled away and went back inside the house without uttering a single word. The prince followed her absentmindedly and came inside as well. He stayed there for four minutes being alone and unrecognized.

Exiting the house he thoughtfully repeated: "The bets are made."

Even the smart neighbors suspected nothing bad: first of all, the prince spent no more than four minutes inside the house, and second of all, the oorijzer of the young Dutchess looked completely in order and undisturbed.

The prince wrote in his diary:

"The isle of Texel (4 degrees longitude, 53 degrees latitude). Bird's eggs. Cheese. Population is friendly. The angles of oorijzers must prick men's cheeks quite painfully. However, the bets are made!.."

The smart neighbors have missed a lot that time: namely, on March 18, 1893 the nice looking soft-faced Dutchess who took off her oorijzer on that occasion delivered a son who was named Jens Boot.

He inherited a high passion for big time gambling from his royal father, that helped him a lot in the future in the business of destruction of one fifth of the world. He also inherited the liking of good milk from his mother, that's why in all those years of wars and revolutions he always kept with him a can of condensed milk made in Middelburg.

4

Further Consequences
of Prince's Careless Attitude

Nothing is known about the early years of Jens Boot except for the fact that he had swallowed a lobster's antenna in 1897 which had upset his loving and caring mother a great deal.

In 1901 we find this gifted boy in Brussels at the cathedral of St. Gudula. He serves there as an altar boy handing the incense burner to the priest, singing with his angelic voice, and delighting the eyesight of Lord Almighty with the pristine whiteness of his laced robes. But his spiritual career is being impeded by his passion for progress. On March 26, 1902 he shows up in the altar wearing bishop's purple soutane, and since this vestment is too voluminous for a nine years old boy it also envelops his childhood friend Jaco-a shoe shiner and seven sparrows. Two boys play ceremonial march with the help of two incense burners and one sauce pan antedating the advent of jazz by many years.

Resourceful Jens was sent to the orphanage of St. Francis where six nuns began to pull his cute pink ears and blond hair off his head, meanwhile weeping and praying to St. Theresa; and then they were helped by father Benedict, who commenced to mollify the sinful flesh with his corny fingers.

Father Benedict did such a great job that Jens's body quickly learned to bend twofold, fourfold, eightfold, and even sixteenfold. That determined his further destiny, and in 1904 he became a pride of Medrano brothers circus in Paris. But his own uniqueness was not enough for that idealist boy. That's why on October 16, 1906 he attempted to bend one of Medrano brothers, namely fat Gaston at least twofold. The results of that attempt were far from satisfactory: it ruined Gaston's plastron as well as the steak eaten by him just before that, and two days later sent Jens on a long voyage aboard "Gambetta" steamer in a role of cook's hand.

Fourteen years old Jens Boot reached the American shore and was delighted: life in Europe from the moment of swallowed lobster's antenna to good old Gaston's ruined plastron was too depressing. But being too young he wasn't certain about his feelings and soon returned to Europe where he was occupied in all kinds of business over the next three years: attended middle school, served as junior barber in Bucharest, picked cigar butts in the streets and entertained public by swallowing burning newspapers.

On July 3, 1910 Ms. Jopple was sitting under her big parasol at the esplanade in Cannes trying to paint the frothy waves of Mediterranean that resembled the weightless seraphs' down with her highly inspired brush. To her utter surprise the figure of Aphrodite Anadyomene suddenly emerged out of the sea froth that on the closer scrutiny turned out to be male, namely Jens Boot, who tried to cool himself in the depths of the sea on that exceedingly hot day. Judging by the pictures that have survived Jens Boot was an exceptionally goodlooking man. No wonder then that the next hour he was having teatime with Ms. Jopple being offered to serve as her regular model.

Ms. Jopple was fifty-eight years old. The proximity of heavenly beauty utterly destroyed her ability to stain canvas with a brush. But that artistic failure had not diminished Jens's manly prowess a single bit. After spending a year with Ms. Jopple Jens decided that his mission was accomplished and, ending the life of that gifted artist with the help of certain chemicals, became the owner of her Riviere villa, pig farm in Yorkshire and guineas at the Bank of England.

But Jens Boot at that time was not in Yorkshire but in Nice, only eighteen kilometers away from Monte Carlo. To that hospitable place he went after mourning the untimely departure of poor Ms. Jopple.

— Eighteen! — shouted Jens betting his entire Riviere villa.

— Eleven, — was polite croupier's answer.

— Eighteen! — Jens repeated stubbornly betting all his Yorkshire pigs

— Thirty-four, — croupier answered with some hesitation.

— Eighteen! — Jens had bet all his guineas that he already had exchanged for francs

— Zero, — whispered the croupier compassionately.

Jens Boot left the casino being a pauper again consoling himself with a thought that he just presented his father with only two hundred and fifty thousand pounds of sterling for the priceless gift of life that he received from him.

Not being too upset Jens Boot acquired a new vocation. He became a hired tango and waltz partner for the ladies over forty. Every day from 5 to 7PM he had to endure their flabby stomachs covered with silk or velvet clinging to him. The ladies weighed from 80 to 100 kilos, and Jens was literally sweating while dancing with them — real Adam's curse. Jens was a really good dancer and oftentimes he wanted to invite some young lady. But that was strictly forbidden by the syndicate of eleven honorable matrons who owned his legs.

All that was going on till January 14, 1914, when something really catastrophic happened, something that hastened the demise of Europe a great deal.

5

Thank you but I don't dance

(On the role of personality in history)

The vulgar opinion of many Americans or Africans attributes the guilt for the destruction of Europe mostly to cunning and soulless Mlle. Lucie Flamengo. Is it worthwhile to dispel such a delusion? Whatever intellectual and spiritual powers that person was endowed with they were most certainly inadequate for the task of turning that great continent into a wilderness. Before even meeting her Jens Boot was thoroughly disgusted with European civilization having gone through a great deal of hardships in his turbulent twenty-one years of life. Moreover, Europe was doomed even without Jens Boot. The war of 1914–18, economic and spiritual disarray of the following decade served as clear signs of catastrophic condition which began long before the creation of the famous Trust Company. But the activities of Jens Boot had no doubt hastened the events by the order of several centuries, and his meeting Mlle. Lucie Flamengo led the great adventurer in its own turn to the most crucial decisions.

This meeting took place on January 14, 1914, as was mentioned before, at 5:30PM in Paris at the establishment named "The Tea Star". As usual Jens Boot was dancing with eleven ladies of the syndicate. But at the aforementioned hour he noticed a young and stunningly beautiful woman with red forelock over pale face. Ignoring all reasons and tradition Jens Boot came to the beauty who just finished dancing with a young diplomat and was drinking her tea. He bowed ceremoniously.

— Thank you, but I don't dance, — she answered with scorn shaking her red forelock and biting on an almond cake with her sharp teeth.

Jens Boot bowed ceremoniously once again and stepped away. And the beauty that turned out to be seventeen years old daughter of the owner of thirty oyster farms and six silk factories was already dancing with someone else. The dames of the syndicate surrounded Jens and squeezing him with eleven flabby bellies chastised him for the breach of contract. Jens went out. He knew that he had fallen in love. He also knew that Mlle. Lucie Flamengo did not want to dance with the poor hireling dancer.

Stopping at the window of Cunard Line shipping company he looked at the map of Europe. Surrounded by the seas the daughter of Phoenician king was still basking.

— Gorgeous continent! — Jens Boot thought. — But everything is designed in such a way here that makes life impossible... Maybe I should move to Africa... There is sand and skies there...

He was about to open the door of the shipping company but then turned and unthinkingly bought an issue of evening newspaper and began to pore through it calmly.

Great ideas need some time to mature.

6
Europe or Mlle. Lucie Flamengo?

There was nothing extraordinary about the fact of reading evening newspaper. On the contrary, Jens Boot used to buy "L'Intransigeant" every day. It was from this newspaper issue bought on August 2, 1914 that he had learned that different states of Europe declared war on each other.

It must be told that Jens Boot was a man without nationality. He believed that the passport has to be changed as you moved from one country to another just as one changed an attire. To be Dutch in Italy seemed as absurd to him as wearing a fur coat in the streets of Naples. He carried a full set of passports in a neat light swine leather case along with his collection of neck ties. He spoke eight languages fluently and when asked about his nationality in intimate conversations replied without a shred of irony — European. Since the declaration of war caught him in Paris, he turned out to be French and was immediately mobilized. For the next three years the life of Jens Boot was as dull and monotonous as that of millions of Europeans at that time. He was dispatched to the battery of 305-millimiter guns and destroyed the invisible adversaries while feeding on cold soup covered with a layer of solid lard.

Only once he was moved by a rather ordinary spectacle. Jens Boot looked at the Somme valley from the top of small hill. Before him was bare devastated land. Jens shuddered like a lover who suddenly saw the face of his young girlfriend looking suddenly aged and exhausted, like a face of an old hag. And since

Jens had studied Greek mythology at middle school, he uttered with bitterness to his comrade corporal Michaud:

— Poor Phoenician princess!..

But Michaud did not understand and just giggled.

For three years Jens Boot did the same as others, but considering his future heroic deeds one might easily suppose that his head was full of thoughts of the sort far from trivial.

In the spring of 1917 Jens Boot hid himself in the steerage of a transport and later landed in Arkhangelsk. In October of that year we see him in Moscow aiming his guns at the Kremlin. Calculating the shells' trajectory he mumbled:

— Let's try it! Perhaps, it can be fixed.

Jens Boot sincerely and diligently tried to fix many things. He was leading operations for the liquidation of various consulates in Moscow, fought against French expeditionary force near Odessa, and for four years his heart was beating against a hard booklet in his breast pocket which was his membership card of RKP (Russian Communist Party).

But in 1921 when the communist government of Russia commenced to install state capitalism Jens Boot who was not a cunning politician but an honest adventurer freed his heart sending his party membership card to the regional secretary, shot three chairmen of the trust companies, four chairmen of stock exchange committees and one bank director, took a required document out of his leather case and departed to the bourgeois countries. Jens Boot much preferred the old-fashioned speculation to New Economic Policy. He bought and sold all kinds of merchandise: stock of different mining enterprises, dollars, jewelry of famous beauties, the hearts of ministers and even some disputed cities like Fiume, Memel, Tchernowitz, Wilno and some others.

By 1925 he became fabulously rich surpassing in wealth the Rothschilds, Stinnes, Luscher and other owners of both industrial and financial capital of Europe. But with his habits of a small business manager wealth was of little interest to Jens Boot.

The only diversion of that melancholic billionaire was travel. Led by some secret instinct he never left Europe but for the whole months on end he crisscrossed it in various express trains. He travelled from one sea to another, from the apple orchards of Normandy to the jasmine gardens of the Golden horn bay, from the dwarf fir trees of Lapland to the orange groves of Messina.

The sunset over the translucent valley glowed through the misty window of a sleeper car. Yes, the red forelock was charming on the pale face of the Phoenician girl abducted by a bull! And when the night covered the world, when the lonely electric moon was lighting the sleeper compartment of the train car rushing from one sea to another Jens Boot the former circus boy at Medrano's, a former Red Army soldier under the command of Budenny and now a billionaire in the purple pajamas — he loved Europe wildly and passionately. Yes, not his motherland, nor the world but just a part of it, delicate fugitive, coveted Mlle. Lucie Flamengo!

(It must be added that Jens Boot never looked at himself in the mirror at night).

In the daytime he saw everything: slaves in his mines, deputies, professors, prostitutes and many more. He also saw his own puffy and sleepy face in the mirror. And in the daylight Jens Boot hated Europe, nursing his hate like a baby under his flannel vest. At every terminal in the world, be it Torneo or Palermo, he poked his head out of the window and felt that disgusting smell of rotting flesh as if an old crone with black rotten teeth breathed in his face. That was the smell of Europe. And Jens Boot understood that Europe is old, repulsive, that it was possible to love her only in the darkness, with your eyes shut, never touching her rough skin. Jens Boot was neither a philosopher, nor a politician. That is why he did not write treatises on the decline of the Old World and did not take part in the meetings of Comintern.

Perhaps, that man was born for primeval life. His mother, although she wore an oorijzer knew very little of the treasures of European culture. She was mainly occupied in collecting the eggs of seabirds in the almost barren isle. From his father Jens inherited only a passion for gambling. Should Jens Boot had gone to Africa at the age of nineteen he would find an adequate application to his proclivities there: he would collect the eggs of ostriches, which are quite nutritious contrary to the popular belief and hunted the kings of the desert, lions, which is not much different than playing roulette, by the way. But he had nothing to do in derelict and corrupted Europe of 1920-s.

Once he was passing through Edinburgh and decided to get married. It was in May 1926.

7

Lord Haig's Family Honor
Has Been Offended!

Old lord Charles Haig never attended the sessions at the House of Lords: he was of the opinion that the laws are composed just for the miserable startups sitting at the House of Commons but the lords ought to be concerned only with family traditions. Lord Charles Haig paid great respect to the horse races while scorning the Parliament's bills. The coat of arms of the Haig clan was embellished with a horse's tail, and that fact determined destiny of every firstborn of Haig family.

Lord Charles Haig owned magnificent stables. But in 1924 many misfortunes befell him reminding the biblical story of Job: his hope was ruined when his prized stallion Jimmy failed to win the Derby Cup, his prized mare Victoria broke a leg and had to shot to put her out of misery, Marshall and Rio perished of glanders. Lord Charles Haig's head turned grey, he became gloomy and had to cancel his regular Easter trip to Seville for the reasons of financial order.

It was then that his spouse (Lord Charles Haig had a wife besides having stallions and mares) sitting by the fireplace and turning the dying embers with the antique tongs while relishing the aroma of wilting cherry-pie whispered:

— But we have Mary!

(That was indeed so — besides the stallions, the mares and the spouse lord Charles Haig had a daughter named Mary.)

Speaking of the daughter the noble lady certainly did not mean that beautiful Mary could replace the late mare Victoria in the upcoming race. No, she pored a great deal deeper in the mysterious Book of Destinies. On the left page of that book the debts of lord Haig were listed whereas on the right one was the capital of one rich foreigner that danced a cow-trot for mere three minutes with Mary just last night at the party at Sir Edward Carlisle's house and for those three minutes had his beautiful eyes of a Greek statue fixed on a waxwork beauty of lord's daughter. The right page of the Book of Destinies moved the lady so much that she dared to utter that historic phrase.

— You forget about the family honor of Haig clan, my darling, — replied the lord indignantly and reverently looked at the ceiling where the coat of arms embellished with horse's tail was.

As a matter of fact, lord's indignation turned out to be short lived: three days later he was looking at his daughter who was dancing five-step with a low birth fiancée and just sighed and thought to himself:

— Charles, you keep forgetting about the tail!

We have some difficulty to find the reasons for Jens Boot's proposition to the daughter of lord Haig with whom he just danced a cow-trot for mere three minutes without exchanging a single word in the meantime. Perhaps, touching her warm and defenseless arm he felt something deeply moving. That feeling was alike the one triggered by melancholic pallor of Mlle. Lucie Flamengo, by the warmth of the fountains of Rome, by the delicate beauty of Swedish skerries warmed by the northern sun. European poets of yore tended to call those sensations "love" but we would rather call it "the sense of Europe."

So, Jens Boot proposed and received a positive answer. Marriage ceremony was scheduled on June 12 and was to take place at the family estate of lord Haig located twenty miles away from Edinburgh.

On that solemn occasion the old castle was decorated with hundreds of horse's tails. They were on the walls and ceilings, of the heavy tapestries and delicate window panes. The crystal wine glasses in the gigantic reception hall had the etched image of the tail as well. The noble lady supervised in person all the preparations of the nuptial bed for the newlyweds, and the pillows were also embossed with heraldic tails. And special groom was combing the tails of the stallions and mares at the stable.

Everybody has arrived except Jens Boot. He was expected to come at 11:00AM. The tower clock and the wrist watch of beautiful Mary showed 4:00PM. The priest snorted and shifted as a race stallion at the start.

Another six hours past, it got dark. But that night has not turned nuptial for Mary. The lady had the pillows of the bed covered so that they wouldn't look so mocking. The servants put away crystal glasses, their clanking sounded like a death knell. The faces of the guests turned from joyful to mournful before they finally left, and Sir Edward Carlisle told his wife in a low voice:

— Not only time is money, but money is time as well.

His spouse could not appreciate the depth of his thought and just sighed sadly.

The castle went empty. Long teardrop ran down the pale face of poor Mary. Lord Haig came to the great hall and looking at hundreds of horse's tails pronounced:

— Haig's family honor has been offended!

He was certainly right.

8

Uneasy Parting

A tall man wearing a macintosh coat stopped at the sign of "The Kaffir Smile" tavern that same day at around 11:00AM. It was usual Glasgow weather: drizzle mixed with soot. The man entered the tavern and ordered a glass of whisky. Dropping his head on his hands he sat there for a while as if at a total loss what to do next.

The tavern was located at the port, and other customers: sailors, longshoremen and harlots — peered at the silent guest with curiosity.

At long last the strange customer yawned so loudly and unexpectedly that hostess started as if from a very loud siren. The yawn was an obvious sign of some crucial decision since the guest suddenly became very animated and shouted to the waitress:

— Another whisky, please! And two sheets of postal paper! And a postcard with flowers!

He began to work then.

> *To the general manager of Jens Boot's estate*
> *Heer Alfred Nieuwgewin in Amsterdam.*
> *Glasgow, June 12, 1926*

Dear Mr. Nieuwgewin,

The present is to inform you that I have decided to liquidate all my business and become a Kaffir.

Since collecting ostrich's eggs etc. does not require any capital investment, I send you along with this letter my notarized will which makes you the inheritor of my entire estate and personal belongings including my favorite purple pajamas.

Good luck.

Yours sincerely,

Jens Boot.

PS. I strongly advise you to marry Miss Haig, her address shown on the reverse of this letter.

To Lord Charles Haig
Ian Castle, Edinburgh vicinity

My highly esteemed lord,

I beg your pardon for my missing the solemn ceremony. I also want you to let know your highly esteemed spouse and daughter my sincere apologies and condolences for all the trouble etc. I just have to say in my defense that effective today I have lost all the rights to my property and personal belongings, therefore I did not dare to make your daughter a life partner of the most unfortunate loser.

I hope that you will not refuse to tell my vanishing dream, that is your dear daughter that is still with you, that those three minutes when I danced cow-trot with her I will cherish to my last breath.

Please, dear lord Haig, accept my most sincere respect.

J. Boot.

The postcard with pansies that the waitress has bought after some hesitation at the shop next door was marred with an ink-blot since Jens Boot was thinking too long about what to write on it.

M-me Lucie Blancafort, nee Flamengo
Carte Postale | 26 Rue du Cherche-Midi, Paris
12.6.1926
I am leaving Europe. That is about all I would like to tell
you.

My fair Phoenician girl, I have failed the role of Jupiter and the bull alike. |

I am drinking whisky being in a gloomy mood. I wish you and your spouse fair weather etc.

"The Kaffir Smile" tavern.

Jens Boot

Being done with those literary exercises Jens Boot went to look for a steamer. He quickly found "Romanic" destined for East Africa. He was ready to board it.

But the prince of Monaco was thinking of a really big game while staying at the house of the hospitable Dutchess. Jens Boot was still full of energy and desires despite of thirty-two years of a very active life and very telling yawn at "The Kaffir Smile" tavern. We have already mentioned the great ideas that were brewing in his head.

— Perhaps it is still worth trying to become a Jupiter or at least a bull? — he thought to himself, smiled, and got off the embarkation bridge of "Romanic."

That did not mean though going to M-me Lucie Blanca-fort at Rue du Cherche-Midi and causing some turmoil at her apartment. No, Jens Boot was born for another sort of game and turmoil!

An hour later we can find him among the passengers of the luxurious liner "Mauritania" destined for New York City.

At 10 PM when lord Charles Haig was still at his great hall "Mauritania" was departing from the shores of Europe.

Jens Boot stood at the stern. Beaming through the late summer dusk the red hair of Europe was still glowing. Jens remembered everything — the smell of the meadows near Moscow and the old gloss of Place de la Concorde in Paris.

It was really unbearable, and the great adventurer blew a kiss to his true lover, to Europe, then sat on the sack of pepper and wept. Perhaps.

9

An Excellent Razor for Twenty Cents!

It is quite impossible to state with certainty whether Jens Boot really wept sitting on the sack of pepper in the darkness. At any rate, even if he indeed had shed some bitter tears on the waxed deck of the liner that was the only expression of his sentimental desperation, — of all human activities mourning was the least characteristic of Jens Boot.

He slept well that night and the next morning he recalled all the events of the preceding day and checked his pockets. It turned out that he was going to America with steerage-class ticket possessing one hundred and forty dollars, no luggage, and no memories. That discovery entertained him a lot and he did not get absorbed with the thoughts why he had traded the life of a billionaire for the travails of an unemployed migrant in the slums of New York City or Chicago. He had no idea about what to do in the New World. Jens Boot was of the firm opinion that philosophizing is the trend for monks who produce "Benedictine" liqueur or Russian intelligentsia and not the business of ignoramuses.

Jens Boot was eating roast beef sandwich, his thoughts being vacant. The gigantic fish stuffed with people was rushing along the ancient well-known path. Water was everywhere of course. Everything looked so poetic. But healthy curiosity sprang up in Jens Boot and he explored "Mauritania" using his skill to bend himself sixteen-fold with great ease.

Three quarters of the steamer were occupied by respectable American families who traveled to the old worn-out Europe in pursuit of melancholy that was useful to their stomachs, just as Europeans of the XIX century traveled, according to popular belief, to the ancient ghost cities, to Venice or Bruges. There were only few very rich ones but they liked the spacy rooms and that is why three quarters of the ship were occupied by only one hundred and forty-eight passengers whose combined wealth was on the order of $12,000,000,000. They danced cow-trot on the four upper decks, rode sailed baskets, applauded female boxing competitions, and shot tame hummingbirds. The lower deck was turned into a skating rink where the sons and daughters of the millionaires wearing purple and emerald-green pants were speeding up on the ice despite the July's heat. The uppermost deck was blooming with Sicilian orange trees and Brazilian orchids. The various orchestra comprised of Malayans, Javan, Liberian negroes and balalaika players from Nizhni Novgorod played in the close compartments of the steamer. Diplomatic waiters were serving morning cocktails.

The millionaires sipped the icy drinks, looked eastward, and smirked. They were recalling some attractions of the dying Europe: the alacrity of French women, the sensuality of family-minded German ones, the mystical temperament of the Russian aristocratic ladies — all of whom were eager to please just for a few dollars left in the vest pocket.

Their wives looked in the same direction with gratitude: they were carrying in their spacious suitcases the humble tributes of Europe — dresses made by the best fashion designers, China sets of various dynasties, heavy necklaces and rings of the princes, countesses and baronesses who were spending their last days standing in the lines at the doors of the pawn shops of Europe.

And finally, the dreamy daughters of the millionaires with their giraffe's necks and elephantine feet turned the jelly of their eyes towards the vanished shores where there were Venuses of Milo, Roman lazzarone and other objects of interest that they thoroughly had drawn on the pages of their suede-bound albums.

One hundred and forty-eight first class passengers unwillingly turned their eyes toward Europe while basking in the morning sun.

The other end of the steamer held 5670 passengers of the steerage class. They were all huddled in a crowded space, but what else would you expect for those 5670 people who owned less than $100,000 combined, whereas just one first class passenger the king of steel mister Jabbs has paid $150,000 for his Moorish style compartment. 5670 people could certainly make enough room for him. They were not the citizens of USA, just measly emigrants: Irish, Polish Jews, Italians, Germans fleeing ten years of war and famine wherever they could. They all have long unlearned to murmur or hope.

The "Blue Star" shipping company took care of all passengers, even of that rabble. 5670 people were sat in a perfect order on the clean painted benches and ate nutritious soup out of aluminum cups that were chained to the tables. Special orderlies dowsed them every now and then with carbolic acid and iodoform using gigantic sprayers. 5670 people looked westward stupidly where the new land was expected to emerge out of the ocean's greenish haze, the land that was difficult and unfriendly, like all other lands of the Earth. Only the babies who could not understand the 116th article of the rules of conduct cried every once in a while, but their mouths were promptly smothered with mechanical clamps.

There was an established border between the steerage and first class – a pole with an inscription:

Attention steerage passengers: do not enter.

The ban was strictly enforced by four Negroes dressed in orange uniform. But Jens Boot being once the pride of Medrano's circus easily slithered past four Negroes. Once he turned in the spacious compartments of the first–class he lost any desire to go back to the bench where there still remained another 5669 people. After a friendly conversation with the manager of bathing and hairdressing salons he recalled one of his old trades and became the chief masseur of "Mauritania."

An unusual commotion happened at 10AM in the lower quarters: the steel king Mr. Jabbs was taking a bath. Mr. Jabbs valued his time a lot and that is why five masters were assembled in a spacious Moorish style bathroom. Mr. Jabbs proudly stretched himself on the floor mat. The barber commenced the shaving, the manicurist trimmed his fingernails, the pedicurist did the same with his toenails, the other barber poured a quinine concoction on his head and Jens Boot began to massage his tight round belly. Mr. Jabbs, having given his body to all those people, dedicated his soul now free from all daily business to the conversation with God for the next quarter of an hour.

Behind him stood the apprentices with perfumes, creams, all kinds of pickups, ointments, hair spray and other stuff. Dozens of silver faucets were shining. Pink water was gently bubbling in the marble bathtub, and no less pink and fragrant soul of Mr. Jabbs was soaring high in heavens.

It all resembled a four-stories building: on the first floor was naked deeply purple Mr. Jabbs. Above him the waiters prepared a hearty breakfast for him and the musicians were rehearsing his favorite potpourri from "La Traviata." Yet higher was "Mauritania"' radio station that was sending a cable to his spouse Ms. Jabbs in Pittsburgh: "Slept well. Great appetite. Europe is nonsense. Shall arrive on Wednesday at 12:47."

And above all of that a pink butterfly—the soul freed of flesh.

The masters and the apprentices—all recognized the magnificence of that edifice and kept reverent silence.

Suddenly they heard the squeaky voice of Mr. Jabbs himself:

— Listen, fellow, isn't this razor excellent?

— Yes, Sir, we do our best!

— And how much does it cost?

— Bought in Hamburg, Sir. Converted to our currency— twenty cents, duties and shipping included.

Then something totally improbable happened. The belly under the fingers of Jens Boot suddenly got bloated as never before. The whole body of Mr. Jabbs turned crimson.

— Soda, please! — he croaked

After drinking a glass of water Mr. Jabbs settled a bit and ordered to be carried to a bathtub. Jens Boot lifted the king of steel and gently dipped him in the pink bathtub.

— Twenty cents! — whispered Mr. Jabbs. — And in that country of ours it costs four dollars. Now I see...

Ninety cents in 1920.

Fifty cents in 1923.

And twenty cents now. And they buy nothing. Those syphilitics of "La Traviata"!

No, the only solution is — to destroy Europe!

So, unfolding the scroll of human history we now may exclaim: how many eventualities!

1. Jens Boot could have easily stayed with the rest 5669 passengers of the steerage class instead of massaging the belly of Mr. Jabbs on July 19, 1926.

2. The barber could have shaved Mr. Jabbs with an American-made razor.

3. Mr. Jabbs might have not engaged the barber in conversation being busy talking to God at that time.

Etc.

But something irreparable has happened. Now Jens Boot knew very well why he was going to America.

10

The Invention Hour

Mr. Jabbs was pacing at his office having his sports coat taken off with his sleeves rolled and with a huge manila cigar in his mouth full of yellow teeth as big as the ones of a horse. Every now and then he turned toward the door with a small window where more or less genial heads were showing. It was the so-called invention hour.

Every Thursday from four to five Mr. Jabbs was lending his ear to the offers of various inventors. Every one of them was given one minute to present the main features of his invention. The inventor was then sent to one or the other laboratory if his offer was considered useful to the steel king's multiple establishments. This hour once a week that was spent listening to sixty visitors was certainly worth the trouble since on average no less than five percent of the offers were bought and patented by Mr. Jabbs.

— I am number sixteen, — the voice in the window announced. — I offer magnetofugal cannons. Heavy shells with the range up to a thousand kilometers. Built on the principal of electromagnetic waves. Highly tempered steel.

— Already manufactured at the plant number six. You are late. Next, please!

— Seventeenth. I offer to advertise the products of the trust company with the help of electric arch lamps. The sounds are transmitted through amplifiers. According to my plan twenty thousand lamps should advertise your products every night in New York City alone.

— Very well. Go to Mr. Tyghen who is in charge of the advertisement department. Next, please!

— Number eighteen. I propose to utilize the energy of magnetic storms in Alaska. I have invented a device that retrieves the magnetic potentials.

— Very well. Go to the lab number forty-seven, open every Monday from

— three to four. Next.

— Death to the steam engine! Death to the steam turbine! I have invented the electric element with carbon cathode. An absolute new industrial revolution!

— Nonsense! Take cold shower regularly.

Mr. Jabbs was so indignant with the cynicism of that madman that he even forgot to say "next" and lost two minutes just to express his indignation and chewing on his Manila cigar. Noticing that cigar was ruined he rang a bell, and the head of the twentieth inventor immediately popped up in the window.

— I propose to destroy Europe.

Mr. Jabbs sat on a swivel stool and began to spin being caught off guard. But number twenty went on calmly:

— Organization of the trust company. Capital of twenty billion dollars. You contribute one third of it. I find another two companions. I serve as an executive director. Complete secrecy guaranteed.

— Are you a madman or an anarchist? — asked Mr. Jabbs and stopped spinning in his seat.

— Not at all. My minute is over. But if you give me another three minutes, I shall show the details of my plan. It is quite doable.

After a moment of hesitation Mr. Jabbs picked up the phone and told his secretary:

— Bring the inventor number twenty to my office. Re-schedule the rest of them from number twenty-one to sixty for the next Thursday. Do not call me.

Jens Boot came in. He looked like a pauper being unwashed, unshaven, attired in rags and tatters with torn shoes on his feet and toes showing up through the holes. Who would recognize in that pauper a billionaire, lord Haig daughter's fiancée the best cow-trot dancer at the balls in Paris — and all that just three months ago!

Jens Boot's attire was not just a masquerade. Arriving ten weeks ago in New York city with one hundred and forty dollars he didn't go to the circus of to the barber's shop. He booked a room at a small hotel, bought a small oilcloth bound notebook and began to fill it with some notes. He told the hostess at the hotel that he is a lyrical poet who writes elegies on mythological themes, mostly on amorous transmutations of ancient Greek gods. The hostess immediately doubled his rent rate after that and those one hundred and forty dollars have moved to the drawer of her chest in no time. Jens Boot moved to lower East side then, sold his attire to one Jewish rag and junk dealer for ten dollars and bought the rags from him for two bucks, and in those rags and tatters he showed up at Mr. Jabbs office, who was perplexed in extreme. For seven weeks Jens Boot led a life of a pauper sustaining himself mostly on corn bread and sleeping on the floors at the Salvation army free homeless shelters. But he stubbornly refused to get any job and spending his days and nights on the park benches and train stations still was absorbed in his mysterious business which he used to call the lyric poetry. Two months later the oilcloth bound notebook was filled completely; Jens Boot swiped a golden pocket watch of one absentminded gentleman (it turned out that the watch wasn't golden after all, just gilded silver), bought a train ticket to Pittsburgh and showed up under number twenty at Mr. Jabbs office on his "Invention hour."

Entering the office of Mr. Jabbs Jens Boot came to his desk, took a Manila cigar, and lit it, then sat in an easy chair crossing his legs, not being embarrassed a bit with his toes showing up through the holes in his shoes. He then took out his oilcloth bound notebook and handed it to Mr. Jabbs.

On the first page of it was written in the neat handwriting of a good pupil:

Organization Plan of the Trust Company for the Destruction of Europe.

The next pages contained not the elegies but the tables, the diagrams and resumes of different plans. Ten weeks were not spent in vain.

Mr. Jabbs stayed at his office with Jens Boot till 11:00PM thoroughly studying all twenty-four pages of the notebook. At 11:00PM he asked tersely:

— When?

— We'll begin in 1927. By 1940 it will be finished.

— How much?

— Your share is one third. The grand total should be about twenty billion.

Mr. Jabbs took out his checkbook. Jens Boot had no pockets to hide the check.

Next morning he went to a department store and bought a number of things that are necessary to a businessman, beginning with pants and ending with electric shocker to scare away pickpockets that might be fishing for his wallet. The obliging salesman also offered him purple pajamas. But Jens Boot declined.

"Pajamas are left in Europe, — he thought to himself melancholically. — Pajamas and M-me Lucie Blancafort, nee Mlle. Flamengo. However, they both a going to perish now. I just need to find two more companions."

11

Reasonable Anticipation
of a Honeymoon Trip

Two weeks later Jens Boot came to NYC office of "Cook & Son" travel agency to inquire on the itinerary of Mexican express. His attention was immediately drawn by a tall melancholic youth and three agents who tried their best to animate him in vain.

After getting the paper with all the details of his inquired itinerary Jens Boot quietly threw it into a waste basket. As a matter of fact, he had no plans of going to Mexico, he just visited all kinds of places and offices such as: banks, bath houses, cafes, trust companies' boards, etc. with some modest but unclear purpose.

So, after getting his itinerary details he approached the melancholic youth.

— A little trip to picturesque desert? — asked the agent sounding like gramophone record. — Well, it is quite simple. You depart from NYC on Wednesday at 11:00, the Saharan express departs on Monday at 8:20. Next morning at 9:40 you arrive to Ben oasis, the best desert resort. All attractions are included: camel riding, Arab dances, sand sports, etc. Boarding discounts with "Cook & Son" coupons. On Wednesday at 10 you go...

— No, that would not do, — sighed the youth with the melancholic expression in his eyes going twice deeper. — I want real desert with no people.

The other agent pulled out a thick volume of itinerary book and began to chatter:

— Very well — Gobi then. By airplane. You depart on Friday morning. Stay in Tokyo overnight. On Saturday at 8:00 PM you arrive to Khentschbad in the center of Gobi. Very few people there. No private houses, nor rentals, just five hotels belonging to "Cook & Son." Magnificent landscape. Rooms with desert view. From there...

— No, not that, — sighed the youth ever louder and took off his sports coat since the room was as hot as Sahara. His example was eagerly followed by three desperate agents, and the third one who was the fattest and the sweatiest said:

— In the mountains there are very few people. I would recommend Himalayas. Excellent climate. Cool air. All doctors highly recommend it to the patient with nervous breakdown. There is a cog railway on the slope of Mt. Everest with sleeper cars. You can book a ticket right here. At the summit there is our hotel "The Spire of the World." Six hundred suites with bathrooms. You depart...

— No, you are wrong. I do not depart at all. I would not bother to see one more "Cook & Son" hotel. Life becomes really unbearable — an inquisitive American has nowhere to go!

With those words the melancholic youth left the agent's desk, put on his sports coat quite heroically and moved toward the door. He was stopped by Jens Boot.

— Just a couple of words. I totally agree with you. I can help. But you will need to postpone you trip for a while. In five years say...

— Well, that's not so bad. I plan to marry in five years. Honeymoon trip. But where?

— The Central European desert.

— You must be kidding! To gawk at the Colosseum? No, this is way too low for Williams Hardyle.

— You misunderstood me, Mr. Hardyle. In only five years you and your young and charming spouse may have a trip to the real desert that is about five hundred thousand square kilometers big and has neither "Cook & Son" hotels, nor any other ones. And by 1940 I would advise you to get ready to travel across the Great European desert — about fifteen million square kilometers.

— Listen, — replied Williams Hardyle irritatingly, — this is a bad joke, isn't it? I care not for politics and your satirical allegories...

— No allegories at all, this is a real practical deal quite worthy of these walls that belong to highly esteemed Mr. Cook and his son.

And Jens Boot gave the youth a brief summary of his plans minding the fact that it was exceedingly hot in the midst of August heat wave in NYC.

— Seven billion for a trip to the real desert.

And since Williams Hardyle happened to be the son of the oil king he could afford the small luxury of that funny honeymoon trip.

Jens Boot now had eleven pockets and an electric wallet guard too. That is why he took the check of the oil heir apparent without any hesitation.

— Just try to make it as deserted as possible — asked Mr. Hardyle cordially shaking the hand of the wittiest of all Cooks in the world.

12
But... But What?

On October 17, 1926 Mr. Twyweight whose early breakfast was mentioned in the beginning of our story was giving his famous speech "On Rational Proliferation" at the small fashionable club in Chicago to the group of Mormon millionaires.

Since all the club members were over the age of fifty it is quite understandable that their interest to the presentation was absolutely impersonal and purely theoretical.

However, there was one guest in the audience who looked about thirty years old but he also yawned and made some notes in his notebook and showed no signs of personal interest in proliferation, even the rational one.

The presentation was a resounding and well-deserved success. After finishing it Mr. Twyweight wiped his forehead with a handkerchief, asked for a glass of water and sat in a dark corner shunning the immodest caresses of world renown.

He was found there by the young guest who had already stopped yawning. He vigorously clutched Mr. Twyweight's soft hand and yelled:

— Magnificent ideas! There wasn't a philanthropist like you in human history! You deserve a monument right now! The seeds of your words will certainly fall on a fertile soil! All states will commence to proliferate rationally in just ten to twenty years, but...

At this point the tone of the guest's voice became somewhat mournful, you could feel hardly concealed tears in it.

— But what? — asked Mr. Twyweight being visibly moved.

— But you forgot about one big continent.

— You are wrong, I thought of rational utilization of Africa. By the strictly controlling the process of conception we may succeed in creating the breeds of a useful work-horse people within one hundred years: a porter-man, a driver-man, a waiter-man, etc., whatever trend you like. In the porter-man we'll put an emphasis on physical strength up to ten horse power along with tiny head, cretinism, complete tameness, and vegetarian diet. The waiter-man should have developed hook-like hands with atrophied tongue and complete lack of sexual arousal, etc. This is a lot more humane than robots that were recently mentioned in "Chicago Tribune" and serves the same purpose. The most important thing is to teach our workers Christian humility. Importation of one hundred thousand work-horse men will do socialism a mortal blow.

— You are a true genius, Mr. Twyweight, — exclaimed the guest excitedly. — Besides the monument we should ask the senate to establish a hundred scholarships, and Arch of Triumph and rename a whole state in your honor. "The state of Twyweight" — sounds great. However, but...

— But? But what? —

— You have forgotten about Europe. —

— Yes, young man, you may be right. I said "young," young but reasonable. It is a despicable part of the world indeed. It doesn't buy my world-renown canned meat and generally speaking...

— Generally speaking, exactly, Mr. Twyweight: Europe resists rational proliferation. Listen to me:

1. They shun any proliferation. Let us take France for example

In 1910 birth rate is less than death rate by 0.2%

In 1923 — by 4.6%

2. Proliferation is random and chaotic by and large due to some neurotic states that are dubbed "love" on that side of the Atlantic, not only they produce no useful

breeds, moreover — they multiply dangerous idlers. It is
worth mentioning that in 1926 there were in Europe:
Poets, artists, men of letters, actors, and other idlers —
2%
Soldiers — 16%
Renters — 4%
Paupers — 6%
Monks (Roman catholic and Eastern orthodox) — 0.5%
Monarchs, courtesans, retinue etc. — 0.3%
Altogether 28.8% of absolutely useless people.
3. The most important thing! The only things that Euro-
peans produce with known consistency are the members
of various criminal syndicates, such as: socialists, anar-
chists, and other scoundrels.
In 1890 there were 3.8% of this kind of malevolent crea-
tures in Europe
In 1922 this number grew to 9.01%
By 1925 it has grown to 18.3%.

Of every hundred of Europeans eighteen and a third are revolutionaries, that is bandits, that is people who scorn property
in one way or another. What will you say to this, my dear Mr.
Twyweight?

— I'll say... I'll say...

But Mr. Twyweight couldn't say anything. His little baby-
like eyes have slightly misted. His heart was bleeding. He kept
a pathetic silence.

His interlocutor found the needed words for him then.

— You wanted to say, my dear Mr. Twyweight that it is necessary to destroy Europe then.

Yes, exactly those words Mr. Twyweight wanted to utter but
could not bring himself to do that. Those wild figures stood
in his eyes. Oh, what a bunch of good-for-nothings! Not only
they refuse to buy his pork filet, they breed rebels! Eighteen
and a third scoundrels per every hundred! That one third was
particularly revolting to Mr. Twyweight. He realized that the
decision has to be made.

Finally, he uttered in a muffled tone:
— You are right, but...
— But what?
— But I am a vegetarian!
And after those words the respected owner of the best meatpacking factory in the world broke into such a Niagara of tears that his cute round belly got soaked.

— You own not only the most brilliant mind and the best meatpacking factory in the world but you also possess the most noble heart, — said the Mormon club guest gently. — This triply noble heart should prompt you with the right answer. Your vegetarianism, your highly humane ideas oblige you to act in the most appropriate way.

Europe is drowning in sin, indolence, and social unrest. It will be an act of humanism of the highest order to turn it into a desert. Three hundred million people will be forever grateful to you when reciting "Pater noster" for the last time. And after that... After that we shall rediscover Europe! We shall settle it with colonists say from Africa and we shall begin to breed the useful types of people in that temperate hospitable climate.

Mr. Twyweight was still weeping uttering only: "But, but..."
The insistent proselyte used his last argument then:
— And if we fail to do this after all Europe will spread this contagion to America. Eighteen and a third percent will turn into eighty percent in only five years. Just think of Russia, Germany, Austria. Just imagine something like USSSA.

With those words Mr. Twyweight jumped up and the Niagara of tears turned into a geyser of rabidly foaming mouth.

— Yes, yes! — he was yelling. — I agree! It is absolutely necessary to destroy it! Tomorrow! Now!

He suddenly dropped on a sofa totally exhausted.
— Destroy it. But...
— But what?
— But how can we do that?
— Don't worry about that. Seven billion dollars. You are the third companion.

Jens Boot (the enterprising guest of the Mormon club could not be anybody but him) went out in the street and felt his wallet where the nice check was resting with gusto.

The preliminary work was done. Now it was time to commence with the execution of the main task.

Jens Boot greedily sucked in April air. This air was of special quality: Chicago was breathing the aroma of pigs and bull's blood. That pervasive sticky-sweet smell sort of reminded Jens Boot of his new vocation.

— We'll remove three hundred and five million people, — he said to himself, — but...

— But what?

Against his will he recalled the European springs, those humble and gentle indoors springs, confusion of the bells ringing, light green foliage of Norwegian birches and the poplars of Avignon, the smoky silence of the cities, where every step of a man in love coming back from a tryst under the gaslight stars says: "Too bad, too bad..."

Too bad, speaking honestly. What exactly do you pity? Hundred centuries? A man in love? Gas light? History? A girl that was left there standing by that ridiculous narrow window and clutching all those hundred centuries in her hand, that ancient warmth of Europe? Her? That is Mlle. Lucie Flamengo, now M-me Blancafort? Somebody you certainly pity...

That was what Jens Boot was thinking near the Mormon club smelling the bloody air of Chicago.

— I shall destroy her... And, nevertheless I love her! Europe!

13
Some Analytical Digression

The inquisitive students of American and Australian schools will most likely start shifting in their seats after reading our story to this point. They will probably ask their teachers:

— Why did Jens Boot decided to destroy Europe?

That is the most insidious question! Many well-respected teachers will blush hearing it, wipe their bald heads with tobacco-colored handkerchiefs and blurt:

— That is none of your business, you silly boy!

Unfortunately, we cannot emulate such a talented pedagogue in our serious work and we ought to at least try to answer that question that was born not only in those cute childish heads but also in the very leveled heads of the esteemed readers of the "History of D. E. Trust Company."

It goes without saying that trying to answer doesn't mean answering it. Despite all it all encompassing strength even science sometimes retreats facing various still unsolved mysteries of human heart. We prefer to list some of the hypotheses proposed by the authors who worked on the history of European demise adding ourselves that these are mere hypotheses that oblige no one.

1. Mr. Horle, professor of eugenics attributes the actions of Jens Boot to heredity. He most thoroughly analyses the influence of the mood of his parents at the moment of conception on the character of the child in his seminal work "Four minutes of the prince of Monaco."

2. The local psychologist Mr. Chawten attributes the activities of Jens Boot to an illness called "adventurism" that was very wide-spread in 1920-s and attained really epidemic proportions.

3. Miss Margaret Auden thinks that Jens Boot was simply an unlucky lover, and since sexual emotions played a disproportionately high role in a decadent Europe, the decline of his love by Lucie Flamengo (that later was legally married to Blancafort) made him so mad that in a paroxysm of that madness he decided to destroy Europe.

4. Mr. Birding states with certainty that Jens Boot belonged to a secret anarchistic sect "Tooksook" the history of which he promises to publish in the near future.

We shall not list the arguments of various frivolous authors that flaunt some ingenious but absurd theories in the magazine articles (for instance some one named Mr. Will tried to prove that Jens Boot had never existed at all, although his trousers' suspenders are still on display at the Museum of History in Chicago).

After familiarizing our readers impartially with the opinions of four scientists we dare to present our own hypothesis without any pretensions to its infallibility.

We think that Jens Boot had organized "D. E. Trust Company" and played an active role in the destruction of Europe just because he was a typical European of his time. It is enough to remember his weeping on board of "Mauritania" and his sighs at the door of Mormon's club in Chicago in order to prove his deep and sincere love of Europe. It was that love with her dark mysterious instincts that made him an executive director of the aforementioned trust company.

At the end of XIX century there had emerged a sense of a special European patriotism. People of different countries: French, Danes, Germans and even some Russians suddenly felt themselves as children of some greater fatherland and they loved it. That sentiment reached its peak in the years of great war of 1914–18.

People bowed their heads in the filial ecstasy transfixed with an image of a common garden that was, alas, wilting, and half-dead.

That sentiment was not an obstacle to Europeans who did their best to destroy Europe. Beginning in 1914 wars never stopped. Europeans were busily and thoroughly exterminating each other. Those that used to admire the beautiful garden now laboriously chopped the trees, stomped on the flowers, poisoned the water fountains.

Europe was possessed by suicidal mania. It would not be an exaggeration for us to say that she had killed herself. And her devoted son Jens Boot who was accidentally born through the absentmindedness of the prince realized the thing that was in the thoughts of millions of Europeans in 1920-s and 1930-s — that is mass suicide.

14
"D.E."

We have given a pretty detailed account of the efforts undertaken by Jens Boot in the organization of the "D. E. Trust Company."

In the end the board of trustees of the company met on April 4, 1927 at the private room of first-class New York restaurant "Missouri". Besides Jens Boot there were Messrs. Jabbs, Twyweight and Hardyle. They talked of many things but mostly of the different brands of cigars.

Mr. Jabbs preferred the Manila brand "Rosa del Oro" made by Lopados factory in Maduro.

Mr. Hardyle's favorites were the Havana "Aromaticos" made by La Corona factory, Colorado.

Mr. Twyweight liked the Sumatran brand "Flore fina" by Bath &Co factory in Claro.

Jens Boot liked the chocolate ones.

However, after discussing the qualities of all sorts and brands of cigars the board issued a following resolution at around 4:00 AM: *Authorize Mr. Jens Boot to commence the execution of the discussed plan.*

We have called the morning of April 11 of that year was an historical one for a reason: three Americans were having their breakfasts, Europe was dozing off in her bath, whereas Jens Boot was issuing orders to eighteen thousand seven hundred and sixty agents of the trust company.

The latter was as invisible and imperceptible as the ruling of the universe by God Almighty. Except that Jens Boot did not have the staff that would be able to match the legions of angels. The small office of the "D. E. Trust Company" was situated on the thirty second floor of an average size high-rise building and contained only seven people: Jens Boot's secretary, two stenographers, two telephone girls, a bookkeeper, and a groom. Of course we have to add Jens Boot himself, who was waving his red-and-blue pencil like and orchestra director's baton of God Sabaoth.

The office had three rooms. The door sign informed:
Engineering Trust Co. of Detroit.

In the first room one could see topographic maps of Detroit on the walls, and the typewriter girl was copying the estimates of the bridge construction work connecting Detroit with Windsor, ON in Canada.

In the second room another typewriter girl was typing letters addressed to various organizations that didn't seem to have any relation to the bridge construction. The telephone girls were busy sending messages which content wasn't quite clear to them (but of course this vocation is valued for its obedience rather than for curiosity).

The bookkeeper was there mostly for decorum. He meekly recorded the profits and expenses of that small engineering company with fixed capital of one million dollars. As for the secretary who incidentally had a university degree in his resume, he had nothing to do with the real activities of "D. E. Trust Co." His duties included conducting negotiations with the local authorities in Detroit, monitoring the exchange rate of US dollar at the European stock markets and purchasing cigars for Jens Boot, both real and chocolate ones. It is now easy to see considering that latter fact that the groom had nothing to do at all and was just sitting on a stool all day long which at his tender age led to him growing prematurely and unfittingly obese.

Jens Boot himself was situated in the third room. There was a big map of Europe on the wall in front of him. Such a thing at the engineering company of Detroit was explained by geographical inquisitiveness of the esteemed director. There were also some tables, diagrams, voluminous summaries, and projects but they all fit in one safe box and nobody new about their existence.

Jens Boot was sitting at his desk waving his red-and-blue pencil and issuing orders to seventeen organizations that had nothing to do with the destruction of Europe but all had "D.E." initials in their names.

Those seventeen organizations were located at different states of America. They in their turn were managing the activities of three hundred and fourteen institutions located in all states of Europe which had eighteen thousand seven hundred and sixty employees combined. Therefore, one motion of a red-and-blue pencil ruled the conduct of eighteen thousand seven hundred and sixty people, and among them were the kings, the presidents of the republics, ministers, owners of the largest trust companies, bankers, chiefs of staff, leaders of political parties, cardinals and even criminals.

It goes without saying that none of those eighteen thousand seven hundred and sixty agents of "D. E. Trust Co." knew or even as much as suspected that they were realizing someone's insidious designs. All those different trusts and societies, parties, and unions of which those persons were members were pursuing seemingly quite different and benevolent goals. They all had different names, such as "Democratic Emancipation League of Europe" or "Daughters of Eucharist," etc., etc. but all had D.E. initials in their seals and letterheads, on their placards and building facades.

In order to imagine the smoothness of "D. E. Trust Co." operations it is enough to recall the panic that broke out in Europe on May 19, 1927. On that day the red-and-blue pencil of Jens Boot was resting on his desk dead as a doorknob. It was due to a tiny but rather pleasant accident: Jens Boot was riding an elevator with some stranger girl. The accident happened between the twenty seventh and twenty eighth floors. All of a sudden, the elevator stopped, the lights went out. The building was equipped with seven elevators, so the doormen assumed that the broken elevator was empty and were in no hurry to call the mechanics to fix it.

The girl being noticeably upset uttered in a darkness:

— I am losing my work day. That is four dollars. I shall sue the building administration for ten dollars. Will you support me?

Jens Boot decided to support her right away rather than delay it for an indefinite period of time. He stretched his arm and not only supported but embraced an indignant girl. We can't say for sure whether the American girl was fully satisfied and happy since it was still dark in the elevator.

Meanwhile the time was passing by with the red-and-blue pencil as well as the phone staying idle and the functioning of different European organizations deeply disturbed. At the stock exchange in Berlin the dollar exchange rate dropped by a hundred points then soared incredulously. The prime minister of Denmark fell ill with nervous breakdown since the Riksdag three times within one hour passed the no confidence vote and three times demanded the resignation of his entire cabinet. Serbian regiments at the Bulgarian border gave something like a show of a square dance penetrating the enemies' territory and then retreating — the army commander general Iovanovic received sixteen different relays from Belgrade, each of them recalling all the previous ones.

The black box was still hanging between the twenty seventh and twenty eighth floor.

Jens Boot was combing his hair with a small pocket comb and was thinking of Europe. But in those minutes his thought had nothing to do with the successes of the trust company. He was totally oblivious to the falling of German mark, to the government crisis in Copenhagen, to the Serbs invading Bulgaria, he was thinking of the other Europe, of a delicate beauty who embraced the thick neck of the red-eyed bull with her weak arms.

Miss smelled of ink, carbolic soap, and soot. Anemones and violets were blooming in Europe. Mlle. Lucie Flamengo preferred Guerlain perfume to all other brands. Miss had skin covered with goosebumps, that was as rough and business-like as sandpaper, and it was abrading Jens Boot's cheeks. Delicate, ever so delicate were the valleys of Ile-de-France...

Jens Boot was absorbed in that comparative ethnography until the absentminded doormen noticed their mistake. Suddenly the lights went on in the box. Miss busily looked at her wrist watch. The elevator had arrived to the thirty second floor. Parting with the girl Jens Boot uttered:

— You are the most beautiful woman of the New World. But I am an archeologist in pursuit of Phoenician.

Miss replied calmly:

— I don't care. Besides the work day I have lost my innocence and I am suing you for ten thousand dollars.

Jens Boot being ignorant about the market value of the aforementioned virtue rewarded the girl generously. Writing her a check he quickly proceeded to his office and took his red-and blue pencil. The telephone girls began to work.

An hour later the German mark finally fell and rested there for good: Germany was to be bankrupted. Triumphant Danish prime minister was lighting up his first cigarette of that tumultuous day: he declined the petition for unemployment benefits, — therefore he was worthy of support.

Serbs smarting their hats entered Bulgarian border town: Jens Boot was no pacifist.

So was it going on May 18. But so was it going on April 18 and on June 18. So was it going every day.

Some touchy-feely philosophers mumbled something about "the fatal blindness" of European politicians, businessmen, diplomats, and capitalists. They were blind themselves and could not see that behind the backs of those eighteen thousand seven hundred and sixty seemingly powerful people there were the shadows of seventeen humble American organizations, and that behind those seventeen organizations — the red-and blue pencil belonging to a director of a measly "Engineering trust of Detroit."

And Jens Boot was not blind. He knew what he was doing. He lied insolently to the gullible girl in the stuck elevator. It was not in a dream but in real life that he was pursuing the Phoenician beauty!

15
Jens Boot's Name Day

On June 24, 1928 Jens Boot was celebrating his name day and there was certainly nothing extraordinary about that. Events like that happened regularly every year. At the time when Jens Boot still lived with his mother at the island of Texel he was presented with the biggest egg of a seabird on that day. In his Medrano's circus years glory he would get the most resounding slap from the eldest of Medrano brothers Gaston on that day. And in his billionaire of Europe years, he would celebrate it with buying himself the most expensive pajamas. Name days have their own history and traditions which we are not going to discuss here for want of time and space.

But in 1928 Jens Boot's name day was celebrated in a very special way, without eggs, slaps, or pajamas. Even the celebrator himself wasn't present. Not a single person in the assembly remembered of the very existence of Jens Boot. It was the most special name day.

On the twenty fourth of June 1928 M-r Felix Brandeveaux, the new head of the cabinet ascended the rostrum of the Chamber of Deputies. Opening his square mouth he exclaimed:

— No more!

And froze. The whole Chamber froze likewise. It would be no exaggeration to say that all France and, moreover — all Europe froze because with all its finality his first word meant nothing whereas the second one would determine the fate of hundreds of million people.

The pause between the first and the second word was very long indeed. M-r Felix Brandeveaux was in no hurry to speak but he was never slow to act on his words. He has reached his high position through no regular parliamentary procedures. No, that sardine cans manufacturer had the blood of great Buonaparte in his veins!

On the eve of Jens Boot's name day, that is on June 23 he came to the doors of the Chamber of Deputies accompanied by three thousand members of the semi-secret union that he himself had organized. The deputies did not want to let him in, and he argued with the policemen for quite a while. Three thousand union members then showed the police in quite friendly manner that despite being politically conservative they were very much for the technologic progress and are quite familiar with the newest achievements of the military industrial complex. The deputies after finding that out hid themselves in the wardrobe room and at the cafeteria yelling:

— Let them in! For God's sake let them in immediately!

M-r Felix Brandeveaux proudly entered the assembly hall. The chairman of the Chamber of Deputies who was found hiding in a far corner of a restroom immediately made a phone call to the president of Republic, and in half an hour m-r Felix Brandeveaux came out to the people assembled in the square before the Chamber as the newly appointed prime minister. Police saluted him politely. The union members dispersed to the cafes and restaurants nearby and were drinking bittersweet aperitifs.

The night of June 23 to 24 was quite unrestful for the deputies, but in those sleepless hours they were thinking a lot and quite fruitfully. By the morning the majority of them began to share political opinions of m-r Felix Brandeveaux very sincerely.

The next meeting of the Chamber was scheduled at 3:00PM for the sole purpose of hearing the new prime minister's declaration.

— No more! — repeated m-r Felix Brandeveaux once more and paused again.

Then, taking pity of poor Europe, whose pulse was quite irregular by then, he finally uttered:

— No more peace!

The deputies jumped up and broke into a wild applause.

— We spared Germany long enough! That insidious country ruins itself deliberately in order not to feed our triply dear motherland. Let us remember the horrors of 1914. Who else but Germans destroyed the Reims cathedral?

The audience was in the extreme ecstasy. The deputies from Reims were weeping and laughing at the same time due to the depth of their feelings.

— We are peaceful people, — prime minister went on, — but we shall reach our goals. We shall apply sanctions. In the next few weeks the hornets' nest of German resistance in Berlin will be destroyed.

With those words the Chamber roared wildly, nothing like that was ever heard in the entire history of French Parliament. That roar was so loud that it penetrated the ancient walls of the Bourbon's palace, reached Place de la Concorde, and shook the ancient Egyptian obelisk.

Deputies were battle-ready. They felt themselves young, vigorous, full of Gallic virtue and Latin intellect.

However, some scoundrels with deputy mandates that sat on the left benches tried to contradict.

— M-r Felix Brandeveaux have chosen the perilous path of national egoism — yelled the most loud-mouthed of them.

But the Chamber managed to tame them quickly without violating the sanctity of the constitution. Within three minutes the Chamber issued an edict to strip all the communist deputies of their mandates, after which those criminals were escorted to La Sante prison. As for the socialists, they were given fifteen minutes to think of their future destiny. The socialists used that time very well and issued two resolutions: one — against the perilous tactics of the ruling cabinet, and another — against the perilous tactics of the communists.

The first resolution they left for reading in the close family circle sending a copy of it to the archives, the other one they announced immediately, and deeply touched m-r Felix Brandeveaux kissed the leader of the socialist fraction on his cheeks that were cold with horror.

After that prime minister went to the cafeteria and humbly asked for a glass of lemonade on ice. The deputies formed a line behind him and shook his sweaty hand. M-r Felix Brandeveaux gave his card with autograph to each one of them. The wallet of prime minister was inscribed with the motto of his victorious union — "Destruction and Expansion" — D.E.

And the deputies rushed to the boutique at Rue de Rivoli to order the same wallets.

Jens Boot must have been pleased with his name day. But he was far away, in Berlin and found out about the session of the Chamber of Deputies only at 9:00 PM coming out of the movie theater where he watched the comedy "Piki Wants to be a Dancer". An old woman at the doors of the movie theater yelled hoarsely:

— Extrablatt!! Death sentence to Berlin!

Berliners read it and yawned. They were used to everything. After reading about the Chamber of Deputies resolution they said:

— That Piki is very funny. He falls so deftly! We'll see his next show "Piki makes a proposition" if Berlin is not destroyed by Friday.

Jens Boot smiled reading the paper:

— Very decent present!

Indeed, it was a lot tastier than the egg of a favorite seabird and more resounding than the loudest slap. As for the pajamas, our readers already know that Jens Boot refused to wear that touchy attire that was forever linked to the intimate moments of his past life once and for all.

16
Pharaoh Pherunkhanun Last Words

—The last train has departed from the Zoo Station an hour ago! — a diligent grey-moustached railway control official at the Friedrichstrasse station announced methodically. He was uttering those words until the mad crowd crushed him to death.

But the crushed official was correct: the last train left Berlin on 29th at 2:00 PM bound for Breslau. Even before its departure all the commuter trains were converted into the long-distance ones. Some of the trains were expected to come back by 5:00 PM and that is why the squares near the railway stations were crowded with people. Some dreamers were sitting on the huge bundles packed with beer steins, pillows, and complete sets of German classics, such as Kerner and Lessing. But it soon became clear that French air force pilots have destroyed all of the twenty-eight railways leading to Berlin. The crowds quickly dispersed then.

Not just automobiles but even the horse-drawn carriages were driven out of the city. The resourceful millionaire Herr Fischer who got stuck in Berlin because his wife was in labor found a broken truck that was used to deliver fish late in the day. Herr Fischer loaded himself and his family in that truck. But some workers stopped the truck near Grunewald, snuffed out Herr Fischer and then broke the truck completely in the ensuing scuffle.

Many decided to leave Berlin on foot. They trudged mostly to the east and south.

Some fell on their way being exhausted. One old Frau was riding a baby pram pulled by a harnessed she-goat. The goat bucked, leapt sideways and finally gored its owner. Some had hired porters who carried them on their shoulders. The cigarette manufacturer Herr Wolfe had hired four porters for a thousand dollars. They were supposed to transport Herr Wolfe and his spouse at the speed of no less than 6 km/h. The sinews and veins conspicuously bulged and pulsated on the porters' necks. Herr Wolfe dozed off on the shoulders of a porter and was sleeping like a baby. But when they were passing the Spree the porters quietly let go of their warm load, and Herr Wolfe and his spouse just stirred the mirky waters for a minute.

As a matter of fact, no one paid any attention to those kinds of accidents. Those that left were determined to survive and therefore were in a hurry. The majority, however, decided to stay in the city.

According to an estimate made by Argentinian statistician Mr. Robes there were still two million and six hundred thousand inhabitants in Berlin in the evening of June 29. Those people had survived a world war, three revolutions, famine, and privation. They had not taken cyanide, nor they jumped into the Spree. But they were ready to die in case some Herr Felix Brandeveaux really insisted on that. It was not because of their politeness but just due to the limitations of human condition.

It must be said that some optimists were still hoping for the miraculous delivery. Consoling rumors filled the city. Some were saying that forty kilometers west of Berlin there were land mine fields that would blow up the advancing tanks; the others were saying that there were batteries of Russian anti-tank guns in the suburbs. All that was sheer nonsense. There were no mine fields and no guns. Just one hundred and eight youths organized "Detachment of self-defense," armed themselves with old rifles and were guarding Charlottenburg, and anticipated the enemy.

At 9:00 PM some resourceful oddball had printed the special issue of "Deutsche Zeitung" full of sensational reports:

Paris. The government of Brandeveaux was overthrown this morning. Paris Council of the worker and soldier deputies salutes the workers of Berlin.

Washington. The President of the United States issued an ultimatum to the French government demanding the immediate withdrawal of sanctions. American public opinion is very much against the destruction of Berlin.

Berliners just smirked kindly after reading those cables composed in Leipzigerstrasse. Perhaps, they believed them for just a minute but that minute lasted for no longer than any other minute and that belief was than dispelled and replaced by the firm conviction that America had no business to care for two million and six hundred thousand people roaming the doomed city, that Herr Felix Brandeveaux with well-groomed moustache still ruled his rabid country and that three hundred heavy tanks were on their way from Hannover to Berlin.

In the evening there still were some political activities. One hundred and eight youths armed with old rifles who guarded Charlottenburg had restored the imperial power. They changed the flags on one of the buildings. But there was no emperor to be found in the city and its inhabitants did not care for the flags. The coup was noticed by no one. An hour later the communists decided to act. They tried to send a radio message to the soldiers in the tanks reminding them of the proletarian solidarity. One of them began to compose a decree: "In the next 24 hours all who possess..." But he recalled then that Berlin had no more than three hours left to live and went to drink Kirschwasser forgetting about his pen. By 10:00 PM no one cared about politics. Even the most devoted jurists didn't give a damn about who exactly held the local authority.

Festive mood reigned in Berlin. Workers and clerks stormed into the luxury apartments of the profiteers that have left the city. They were not rummaging their chests for valuables and they weren't smashing the mirrors. They only took the delicacies, the wines from Rhine and expensive cigars. Some women tried to play the pianos and wept. Maybe those tears were the sign of joy.

At Kurfurstendamm one fanatical cabaret owner who obviously believed in his personal immortality resolved to make a fortune. He had hung a huge placard:

Al CASAR CABARET
THE LAST NIGHT OF BERLIN
Everybody hurry up! It is not too late!

There were no actors, they all ran away. Including the animal tamer and clown Dimas. The owner put on a woman's skirt embossed with glass beads and began to give the show himself: he danced cow–trot, sang frivolous satirical songs, juggled with plates, and even impersonated an elephant and tamed himself quite successfully. The audience was quite large.

Berliners obviously wanted to relax and enjoy that last night. The crowds stormed the movie theaters and opened the shows on their own accord. But since there were only the amateur mechanics the movies were running either wildly fast or extremely slow. The lovers kiss in one of the movies lasted for no less than an hour. But it did not surprise anyone. The movie watchers realized that that was the last kiss and kissed each other for just as long. In the other movie pedestrians were running with unimaginable speed, and the watchers seeing that ran into the street and rushed on knocking off each other: after all they had only another two or three hours to live.

All restaurants, cafes, beer halls, sweet shops were full. Waiters were sitting at the tables sipping champagne. The customers helped themselves. No one gave a damn about money. Musicians were still playing as usually.

Dreamy and drunken people roamed the streets. They recited poems and swore with no malevolence. Red and yellow lights were glowing in the verandas of cafes. Dry tinny sounds of people kissing were heard everywhere.

Some noseless cripple seduced a naïve girl with a billion marks and a chocolate bar. It was too far to walk home and the time was running out, so they laid on the lawn in the nearest square. A stray dog came close, sniffed them, and uttered a melancholic howl. The howl was muffled by a jazz drum. Above the drum the overgrown orange of the moon was swinging slowly. Literature connoisseurs said that it all reminded them of Hoffmann.

The time was running on, it was midnight. Suddenly all Berlin squinted because of the unbearably bright light. Gigantic searchlights were piercing the city. A girl that was lying on the lawn jumped and ran away. An old German brought out a thick volume — "The History of Frederic the Great" — put on his horn–rimmed eyeglasses and began to read out loud. A dog kept howling.

A new guest entered café "Prager Diele" yawning gloomily. There were no vacant tables left. He came to an old, grey–haired gentlemen who was sitting at the table by the window, bowed politely and asked:

— May I?

The café was full and joyful. Some merry fellows brought paper streamers and their orange cobweb was covering women. But the new client just looked impatiently at his wrist watch like a nervous passenger spending a night at the connecting station. It was Jens Boot.

3000 tanks were already within 25 km from Berlin. In one of the tanks there stood two friends, they were naked due to unbearable heat — lieutenant Victor Brandeveaux, the prime minister's nephew and second lieutenant Jean Blancafort. The tank was crawling at good pace smashing small groves, piercing the walls of old churches, traversing ravines.

— It is hot, — said Victor Brandeveaux, — awfully hot! Just like Nice. And people are naked as if on a beach. Look, we just have smashed a big house, there is a baby's crib and a boot sticking out of the hole in the wall. That must be Berlin's suburb.

Jean Blancafort was in good mood but the crib and the boot were of no interest to him. In his opinion mobilization and annihilation of Berlin was a refuge from the daily arguments with jealous Lucie and home-cooked veal that was sickening to him. He shared his ideas about the future pleasures with his buddy:

— In Cologne one franc was worth four million marks. They say that you can find the nicest girl in Berlin for only ten million. So, let's work tomorrow, right?

— But you have forgotten that in an hour we shall destroy Berlin with all its inhabitants, — replied Victor Brandeveaux.

A searchlight illuminated the steep walls, the chimneys, the bridges, the water towers. 3000 tanks formed a chain that was supposed to level the whole city.

Victor Brandeveaux spoke again:

There is a lamp in the window. You know, Jean, it's quite awful! As if we drove for a long, long time for not kilometers but millennia. Ran with our tongues out. And now here is the end of it, a wasteland with a broken lamp. I feel time very acutely right now. As if there is a chronometer in my chest instead of a heart.

But Jean Blancafort said nothing. He noticed hundred and eight youths armed with old rifles who tried to attack the impenetrable armored monsters and ordered to mow them down with a machinegun as well as anybody else in the streets who tried to escape.

The west end neighborhoods were already turned into rubble, but at "Prager Diele" a joyful violinist with black eyebrows was still playing Peruvian cow-trot. The venerable gentleman finished his cup of ersatz acorn coffee and told Jens Boot:

— I am very upset with what is going on. The matter of fact is that I shall most likely perish in the next quarter of an hour. I had no time to tell anyone about my last work. For three years I sat in my study. I have not seen anyone all that time. I did not even know that there was going to be another war. I was deciphering the inscriptions of the tomb of Pharaoh Pherunkhanun that was discovered in 1925. It was only today that I finally have deciphered the final line: "In the very end there is a beginning."

Those were the last words uttered by the Pharaoh, who lived in XII century B.C., that is 3300 years ago. But I have discovered this too late. It seems like the mail isn't working already. I am about to die, and nobody will know what were the last words of Pherunkhanun.

At that moment they heard the thundering rattle of collapsing buildings. Two tanks having already destroyed all the buildings in Keiserallee moved toward Pragerplatz. Cow-trot suddenly stopped. The wine glasses fell on the floor. Some of the guests rushed toward the door crushing each other. The others kept sitting paralyzed with horror.

Venerable Egyptologist stayed calm and asked Jens Boot:

— Despite of your dismissive attitude to my work I dare to ask you a favor. If you survive me, please, take this sheet of paper out of my wallet that contains the most accurate translation of the inscription at the tomb of Pharaoh Pherunkhanun and send it to my daughter Fraulein Ilse Krieger in Nuremberg, Munchenerstrasse, 11. She will report my discovery to the foreign scientists. Do it for the sake of humankind.

Jens Boot smirked ironically but nodded his consent. A woman who fell on the floor was crying wildly. The next minute everything was engulfed in a stony tornado. Jens Boot and the Egyptologist both fell to the ground. A tank moved on victoriously moving its guns like beetle's antennas. But Jens Boot and his learned interlocutor Herr Krieger were still alive. Jens Boot had thoroughly shaken the dusted cement off his coat and lit a cigarette. Stone rubble and corpses were everywhere. Getting from under the rubble they saw a few mad people who were jumping from one stone to another. Among them was the owner of Al Casar cabaret in his skirt glistening with glass beads. Holding and supporting each other Jens Boot and Herr Krieger staggered away. Jens Boot knew with certainty that he would not die, since "D.E Trust Co." had merely begun its work. He looked at the golden dust of the stars and thought of the letters that he had to send to Paris tomorrow.

One of the tanks was getting closer to them.

Herr Krieger told Jens Boot:

— Don't you understand who needs the inscription of the tomb of Pharaoh Pherunkhanun? You, me, that man in a skirt, soldiers in the tank, everybody, absolutely everybody! I see a long black tunnel of the millennia. It is behind us. You do remember the words of Pharaoh: "In the very end there is…"

Herr Krieger could not finish that consoling aphorism of Pharaoh Pherunkhanun. He fell hit by a bullet that flew out of a narrow barrel of a machinegun. In the tank stood Victor Brandeveaux and stared vacantly down the long black tunnel of millennia with glassy eyes.

17
When Almond Trees Bloom

Jens Boot did not care at all for the aphorisms of the XVIII dynasty Pharaoh, as we have seen from the previous chapter. But our protagonist was known for his scrupulous honesty: he was true to his word.

It was gorgeous summer day. Disheveled women and men with their neckties flying behind them were running in panic down the nice lawns and meadows of the Spree valley where just few days ago busy Berliners used to spend their restful weekends. They ran yelling wildly, tearing their clothes against thorny bushes, squatting and falling, they ran like wild animals run away from a wildfire. Those poor people were the lucky ones indeed, they have managed to escape being crushed under the tanks and were not killed by the hail of bullets.

About eight thousand Berliners survived m-r Felix Brandeveaux's first sanction.

Among them was Jens Boot who walked leisurely holding small worn-out briefcase. He was true to his word. Not only he promised Messrs. Jabbs, Hardyle and Twyweight to destroy Europe, but he also agreed with a nod to execute late Herr Krieger's last will, that is to deliver a paper with the last words of the aforementioned Pharaoh to Fraulein Ilse.

Of course, it was a lot easier to nod than to reach Nuremberg in Germany that was engulfed in horror, but Jens Boot was not stopped by any expenditures, like any firm that cared about its reputation.

By noon he reached a village of Bitterfeld, spotted a motor-cycle at the door of a cigar shop and drove south without waiting to talk to its owner.

Germany presented a really bizarre spectacle at that time. French air force had already wiped out several cities: Stuttgart, Dresden, Breslau, and some others, besides it had damaged the railways which all but stopped the train commute.

The cities that still survived were isolated and led their own lives or, to be more precise, were getting ready to die each in its own way.

When Jens Boot reached Leipzig, the city was in the midst of civil war. Leipzig's socialists still defended the authority of the central government in Berlin although the latter had already perished under the tracks of French tanks. The communists of Leipzig were against it and demanded the all-Germany assembly of the factory workers councils. The battle lasted all day long. By late evening communists prevailed. Next morning the solemn funeral of the victims of revolution was scheduled. However, Leipzig was wiped out by French by about 2:00 AM.

Jens Boot moved from Leipzig to Halle. Unlike Leipzig the city was absolutely calm. The influx of refugees from the ruined cities has revived commerce considerably. All the sweet-shops were full to the brim, and the tallest Baumkuchen as big as hundred years oaks were consumed in a matter of few minutes. The city council was debating a new tax on dogs. An orchestra in the public park was playing potpourri from Meyerbeer operas, at 9:00 PM maids took out four thousand tax-paying dachshunds for a necessary stroll. At nachtlokal two forty years old beauties sisters Emily and Minna Leiser were dancing completely naked. They smiled amiably and smelled of sweat. Halle was also wiped out on the night of the 1st to 2nd of July.

The gangs of "self-defense" made up of disabled men and schoolboys were roaming the country. Not finding an enemy they shot the skies with their rusty 1914 vintage rifles. Scared women fell to their knees pleading with those defenders:

— Please, do not irritate him! There is... there is... Herr Felix Brandeveaux!.

There were lots of crazy women as well as men. They fed on turnips.

Some read the bible, since there were no newspapers anymore.

Jens Boot rejoiced having reached Bamberg. First of all, he managed to send some business letters to Paris, Warsaw, and Bucharest. Second of all, he found a real train and that train was going exactly where he wanted to get, but his motorcycle has broken down by then. Bamberg's inhabitants were optimistic and assured him that Nuremberg was perfectly calm.

Jens Boot went to a restaurant car of the train, ordered a schnitzel, and dreamed of the old times when he travelled across Europe not thinking about "D. E. Trust Co.," just studying the landscapes and customs of different countries. He had his purple pajamas then. He wondered if m-r Jean Blancafort was happy with his gorgeous spouse.

With those kinds of thoughts Jens Boot was eating his Wiener schnitzel. The gothic spires of Nuremberg's churches showed up already. Jens Boot loved that city and despite being a director of "D. E. Trust Co." was glad to find out that the Bambergers were correct: French have not yet leveled Nuremberg. He would be able to roam its ancient streets and pass to Fraulein Ilse Krieger the last greeting of her late father.

It was a crispy clear morning. The night rain has passed and therefore the silhouettes of the factory chimneys, the church spires and sharp angles of the building facades looked especially clean-cut on the backdrop of blue skies.

The platform was completely deserted. No porter could be found by the passengers. There was a stationmaster's aide sitting on a bench. He was sound asleep apparently, since he didn't stir even with the train's stopping clang.

Jens Boot who liked the order came close, put his hand on man's shoulder and called out loud: "Wake up, please, dear stationmaster's aide!"

But Herr stationmaster's aide could not fulfill Jens Boot's wish.

All the passengers saw it and rush back in the train cars that they just have left a minute before. Apparently, they had no more liking of Nuremberg left. The train issued a quick whistle and began its journey back to Bamberg.

But the train had left Bamberg at 7:00AM and returned at 11:00 AM. Four hours was a long enough time: Bamberg was no more. The train moved back and forth for quite some time and finally stopped in an open field. A fat Bavarian wearing a Tirolean hat came out of the second-class car, finished off his last sandwich and wept.

When all the passengers hastily left Nuremberg for Bamberg there was only one man left on the platform not counting the stationmaster's aide (and we would not count him). It was Jens Boot. He promised to pass the paper of Herr Krieger to his daughter Fraulein Ilse.

At 9:00 PM the day before Jens Boot's arrival to Nuremberg Ilse Krieger was standing at the balcony of her small house at Munchenerstrasse, 11 and smiled.

Geranium was blooming on the balcony. The stars were shining above and the churches' bells were singing melodiously. But all those things were not the reason for Ilse's smile. Next to her stood the toy store clerk and yet unknown young poet Hans Muller. The smile was very fitting to blonde clear-faced Ilse, it made her look like Swabian Venus painted by Nuremberg master of XV century. Ilse smiled at Hans and Hans smiled at Ilse.

We have some difficulty imagining the mores of perished Europe. How could young people spend hours just smiling at each other senselessly when they were not engaged in some work or sports activities and were not asleep — remains a mystery to us. Such phenomena may be obviously attributed to the already mentioned mental disorder that was called "love." Ilse said:

— The neighbors gabbed about Berlin being destroyed. Does it mean that we all shall perish?

— Yes, Ilse. We most certainly shall perish. But I love you, Ilse!..

He cast down his eyes. Ilse also cast her eyes down. They stood in silence. The stars shone. The bells were singing.

Ilse took a watering pot and sprayed the geraniums with dew. Hans then began to recite his last poem:

> ...In humming lips there's so much of hindering,
> That even if the steel's to atoms blown,
> There still remain a woe and a wafting,
> And rosy almond, and a hefty stone...

But he cannot finish because his lips were too close to the rosy lips of Swabian Venus. The kiss lasted long... Tilting her head back and looking at the stars Ilse whispered:

— It was like your poems. Listen — there are cicadas chirping.

The skies were full of some light silvery humming indeed. They kissed again. Holding Ilse in his firm embrace Hans replied:

— Yes, this is the southern night. Listen- there are almond trees blooming.

It was not a poetic metaphor. Ilse also felt the smell of bitter almond.

— Ilse dear, do you hear me?..

But Ilse was silent. She couldn't possibly answer and Hans could not repeat his question either.

All that happened at about 10:00 PM. And at 9:00 AM next morning Jens Boot left the train station and went to look for Munchenerstrasse.

He entered a café near the station. The customers slumped in their seats. Some were lying on the floor. Unfinished beer steins were shining in the morning sun. It seemed like a morning after drunken orgy and all the people were drunkards being sound asleep. But Jens Boot just saw the stationmaster's aide up close and made no attempt to wake up the customers. He left.

In the square near the station there was a car with motionless driver. He drove it.

The city was nice and quiet. The shingled red roofs shone joyfully.

Every now and then Jens Boot stopped and entered the houses. At the toy factory the workers were resting near the unfinished dolls. It was the night shift. One was kissing a plush teddy bear.

A couple was sleeping in their bedroom: a husband with his nightcap on, a wife with her caul. A clock on a bed stand was still ticking and showing 9:40.

At the casino nine people sat at the table dropping their heads on green baize. Piles of bills showed that one brunette was very lucky. He had just hit the jackpot with his nine.

Jens Boot found Munchenerstrasse in an hour. Stopping at number 11 he saw two lovers still embracing each other. They were hanging over the balcony's siderail. But Ilse's blackened face looked nothing like the one of Venus and Hans's thick purple tongue was sticking out of his mouth.

Jens Boot could not fulfill Herr Krieger's last will. He was late by exactly twelve hours. At 10:00 PM six hundred French pilots dropped their payload on Nuremberg, and Fraulein Ilse Krieger shared the fate of the other four hundred and twenty thousand inhabitants of the city who perished in a space of two minutes.

The city was empty or rather full of blackened quickly decomposing corpses. The July's warm sun was hastening the process of decomposition and the stench of it made Jens Boot to choke. He rushed his way out of the city.

Suddenly he saw a live man in one of the streets. It wasn't a ghost, just an ordinary man smoking his pipe. Catching up with Jens Boot he took his leather cap off and shared his astonishment:

— What a story! Just imagine, I was working as usual. I work with sewage. Not the most pleasant vocation, you know. It stinks — that's the main thing. But one gets used to it. So, I worked down there and I get out in the morning and... there is not a man around! Even the contractor who hired me is dead. What an awkward situation! No one has any use for sewage anymore, obviously. I am unemployed now.

— You are a jolly fellow, — Jens Boot told him. — You shouldn't stay in Europe. I shall send you to America with some mission. You will bring this letter to Mr. Twyweight in Chicago and you will find a job there that fits your vocation. You will get a thousand dollars for the travel expenses.

A man took his cap off again, then put it back on and took it off once more: he agreed.

Jens Boot wrote to Mr. Twyweight:

— I am sending to you a paper with the exact translation of the last thought of some Pharaoh Pherunkhanun. The translator Mr. Krieger passed away on June 28 of this year in the midst of grave incidents that took place in Berlin. As for the Pharaoh, he died three thousand and three hundred years ago. I send this to you because you are the liveliest man of our time.

Today I have explored the city of Nuremberg. There are lots of curious and quite didactic things there. I saw a pair of lovers on a balcony that still embraced while being dead.

I am well and vigorous, and I work tirelessly.

A month later Mr. Twyweight thought after reading that letter: Pharaoh that died three thousand and three hundred years ago was not a fool, as it may seem. The end of one undertaking always means the birth of the other.

Mr. Twyweight wrote in his notebook:

To do:

1.Elaborate on the thought of Pharaoh
2. Pray for the soul of Mr. Krieger

Then, after some thinking he added:

3.As for the dead lovers — they ought to be condemned and forgotten.

18
"Dayosh Yevropu"

In its December 31, 1930 issue "Daily Mail" has published a summary of the most important events of last year:

1. Germany finally ceased to exist. Out of fifty-five million inhabitants no more than a hundred thousand survived. There is now a gigantic wilderness stretching from the Rhine to the Oder that is roamed by gangs of bandits.

Communication between western and eastern Europe is maintained along Paris — Basel — Vienna — Warsaw — Moscow line.

2. M-r Jean Blancafort got fabulously rich thank to his friendship with prime minister's nephew and presented his spouse M-me Lucie Blancafort, nee Flamengo with palazzo in Venice that formerly belonged to Marquis Fermucino complete with all its staff and decorations that is with a beautiful gondolier, mandolin players, Veronese paintings, and excellent bed linen.

3. The meeting of "International Congress of Workers' organizations for the prevention of final destruction of Europe" took place in Zurich. Solemn resolution of protest has been adopted. German delegate comrade Grienbach suggested more decisive measures but his suggestion was rejected: English workers who enjoyed the flourishing of English industries due to the destruction

of Germany were in amiable mood, and the French, all of whom were mobilized, were prohibited by constitutional law to participate in any political activities. As for comrade Grienbach he unfortunately did not represent anyone beside himself since Germany, as was mentioned above, has ceased to exist.

4. Jens Boot admired m-r Felix Brandeveaux's performance so much that he presented him with bronze paperweight made into exact copy of Pharaoh Pherunkhanun's tomb.

5. British prime minister Sir Breadway made a speech at the banquet organized in his honor by the "League for Democratic Emancipation of Europe" where he said that the sole threat to peace in Europe is posed by Russia.

6. Sardine harvest in France was much lower in 1930, and m-r Felix Brandeveaux does not regret the fact that he came to the Chamber of Deputies uninvited three years ago.

7. On Christmas holidays Warsaw and Bucharest welcomed representatives of the "Society for propagation of French culture." There were festive performances. Poles danced mazurka. Romanians played guitars. French guests applauded and had dinner.

The New Year's issue of "Daily Mail" resume ended with joyful accord:

"Despite some difficulties Europe moves toward Renaissance at great pace.

Happy New Year, dear readers!"

The New Year's issue of "Daily Mail" was punctually delivered to the subscribers on December 31, 1930 at about 7:00 PM.

Jens Boot at that time was strolling in the snowy streets of Moscow. He was in festive mood and was eager to reply to good wishes of "Daily Mail" faraway editors with Russian:

— S Novym Godom! S novym stchastyem! (Happy New Year! May it be lucky to you!)

Moscow was getting ready for a New Year. Moscow also was in festive mood. And there were reasons for that. Major administrative and financial reforms that were undertaken last year have stimulated Russian industry considerably. Record harvest helped to close deficits of the preceding years for good. The western parts of the country still have not recovered after the war of 1925. Saint Petersburg has lost its imperial glory and turned into provincial town settled mostly by archeologists, invalids of revolution and aging ballerinas. It must be said that the destruction of Germany has dealt a serious blow to the Republic's economy. But by 1930 Russia began to reorient toward the East.

Siberia was the richest and most powerful part of Russia. Thank to American capital investment and the energy of Siberian natives that part of Russia that was harsh and depopulated, and served as a place of internal exile just twenty years ago now has surpassed Canada. Irkutsk and Chita were as vibrant and growing as many American cities. As for Vladivostok it was already quite clear that in twenty years it would rival San Francisco. In reality Russia began at Volga.

Moscow was an oddity: gigantic densely populated center, the capital city of Republic ruled the Asian part of Russia as if it was the colony. In reality it was a border city, because to the west of it lied devastated and sparsely populated areas.

However, Moscow was still a capital. "Underwoods" were clanking at the trust companies' offices. Shops boasted with goods, schools — with their professors, restaurants — with wines. New Year promised luck and good fortune to everyone.

There were even rumors about the reconstruction of the devastated western provinces. One large Siberian trust company was working on the project of the development of the marshlands of Pinsk.

Only the pessimists who still remembered the years 1920 and 1925 looked at the western neighbors suspiciously. The experiment of m-r Felix Brandeveaux that he made with Germany seemed to teach them very important lesson. But they were pessimists after all.

Population at large stayed quite calm. The western borders were well guarded. Besides, just recently at the reception of the delegation representing the "Society for propagation of French culture" both prime ministers — m-r Tscheteschewski of Poland and m-r Grohotescu of Romania announced their peaceful disposition.

So, Moscow had all the reasons to meet the New Year being well composed.

At the office of the fishery trust company citizen Ilyin was checking the report and company's balance. He was smoking black Manila cigar and looked very much like American king of steel Mr. Jabbs. Unfortunately, citizen Ilyin did not have a swivel stool. But that was the only shortcoming. Just like Mr. Jabbs citizen Ilyin lived by the second hand of his wrist watch, thought only in numbers — millions of tons of fish or billions of rubles, swung his arms and legs while falling asleep because he dreamed of going to the board meeting of the trust company and in that dream he was signing a monstrous bill and demanded the Head of the Skies to pay the estimate of Head of Waters for the maintenance of the trillion kilos of the Head of Fish. That was all a dream, however in reality citizen Ilyin was an exemplary practical person.

Finished with the report and balance he smiled with satisfaction:

Excellent year, and in France all the sardines keeled over. Quite a contrast!

After that citizen Ilyin has scheduled the coming night: from 11:30 till 11:59 two steaks and parfait, at 12:00 — celebrating New Year, 12:01 to 12:14 — toasts, 12:15 to 12:30 — rest and coffee, from 12:30 to 12:42 car ride from Petrovka to Arbat, from 12:43 to 1:00 — making love with a pleasure girl. Then — sleep.

And since the wrist watch was showing 11:23 already citizen Ilyin quickly rolled downstairs and stormed out. One old woman shuffling past the entrance door was shocked and crossed herself.

— Almost knocked me off, God help us! Merican!

Citizen Ilyin arrived at "Eccentric" restaurant just on time. The bosses of all trust companies of Moscow used to meet there. They busily devoured three or four steaks ignoring the sauces. Only the drinking habits still reminded of old European tradition — everybody saw it as a duty to drink French champagne against their will that forced them to snort and spit it out since deep inside they would much prefer good old pure undiluted spirits.

Citizen Khatyan surpassed everyone. He ate eight steaks, drank five bottles of champagne, and hired eleven pleasure girls. At midnight when the second hand of the clock was at 60, citizen Khatyan rose and sang the anthem of the Republic:

Arise ye workers from your slumbers, Arise ye prisoners of want.

Everybody followed his example and stood up promptly still chewing their steaks and gulping champagne. The same anthem was sung by the rebels, the dreamers and ascetics who assembled in the Comintern Hall at comrades' party. The German communist delegate comrade Hackel made a speech:

— The madness of dying bourgeoisie and indecision of the proletarian leaders had already ruined Germany. But this is imperialists' Pyrrhic victory. We may look in the future with composure and confidence. At the international congress in Geneva our resolution had won the approval of one sixth of the delegates. Proletariat is getting rid of illusions by and by.

All who were present rose their beer glasses and cheered. The chairman of French communist party comrade Laurence shook the hand of comrade Hackel firmly and assured him:

— Revolution in France will happen sooner or later.

(As the readers will see in due time, he was quite right and we would even call him a prophet but for the knowledge that sooner or later everything happens in this life.)

Jens Boot wasn't present at the Comintern party, nor at the "Eccentric" restaurant.

Floor waxer Choog, the former red army soldier under Budenny was sitting at a small cooperative tearoom in

Shabolovka street and sipping some translucent and spiritual beverage out of a teacup. A man in a leather jacket approached him and said:

— Don't you remember me? We were fighting the whites together. Long time ago. Some dozen years have passed.

Choog could not boast good memory but he was heartily glad to get a drinking companion and asked for more moonshine.

The director of "D. E. Trust co." had resolved to revive the old custom. In Moscow he felt himself young once again recalling the times when he was aiming cannons at the Kremlin and hoped to save Europe with those innocent shells.

That is why he was celebrating the New Year's Day at the tearoom in Shabolovka street with the floor waxer Choog. Choog uttered after finishing off a third cup:

— So, you say that we beat Denikin together? Alright! And I also beat the French near Odessa... And Poles as well... "Dayosh Varshavu!"

Jens Boot just sighed languidly and asked:

— And how are you doing now?

— Now? Not bad, getting better by and by.

Jens Boot could not find out any details of that "by and by" because their peaceful dialogue was interrupted by a deafening bang.

They ran out in the street together.

— The storage depots have exploded!

— No, that is just the fireworks saluting the Congress!

— These are military maneuvers!

— Goodness gracious, these are the Polish air force!

All kinds of rumors circulated in the crowd. But reaching the Moskva-river Jens Boot and Choog saw that the 4th textile factory was turned into rubble. The Stone bridge was also damaged. The whole Moscow that was peacefully celebrating New Year's Day just fifteen minutes ago was now in the streets in sheer panic. No more arguments were heard, everybody knew that that was the enemy's air raid.

The second and then the third explosion were heard. The power station was destroyed and the city was engulfed in darkness. The chief of Republic's general staff comrade Petrovsky was issuing orders calmly. He was convinced that in a few minutes Soviet air force would repel Polish forces.

The explosions continued. Krasnaya Presnya has ceased to exist. The air force staff reported that the pilots could not find the enemy. Petrovsky squinted feeling at a loss and looked in the window. The explosions continued in the south now, that was the end of the neighborhoods lying beyond Moskva–river.

Commissar of the artillery courses Lukyanov stormed in the room and yelled:

— This is no air raid; it's an artillery barrage!

— Are you mad? Barrage? From where?

Nobody knew. Local authorities in Smolensk and Bryansk were asked over the phone. Their answer was: everything is quiet here, there are no gangs. Petrovsky spoke to Bryansk himself at 2:26 AM. Three minutes later he was killed by another explosion.

Most of the city's population was able to escape since there were intervals between the explosions. All the suburbs along the Kazan and Nizhni Novgorod railway lines were crowded with people.

Jens Boot and Choog were still staying together and warmed themselves by the bonfire at the Bykovo station that morning. Explosions continued even though Moscow was already turned into gigantic wasteland strewn with stone rubble.

No one knew the cause of that catastrophe. An old woman that escaped by sheer miracle mumbled something about that miracle: Moscow perished in punishment for the death of the last priest that happened in the town of Kovrov.

One learned worker-student was yelling:

— These are nitroatomic bombs. Radioactive decay. H. G. Wells wrote about them twenty years ago!

He was yelling that with such a zeal that the old woman pleaded:

— Calm him down, for goodness' sake. It's unbearable. Worse than the bomb.

One plain fool said:

— That's an underground plot.

Choog asked Jens Boot:

— And what do you think this is?

But Jens Boot was sipping his tea and said nothing. The explosions resumed in the evening. They were moving in the same direction the fleeing people were going, that is eastward. Refugees were avoiding major roads an were sinking in deep snow. About two thirds of them perished along the way, the rest have reached Volga.

The Council of Peoples' Commissars surviving members have moved to Nizhni Novgorod that was made a provisional capital. They managed to establish communication with some cities. It turned out that Saint Petersburg, Kiev, and Odessa have perished. Siberians insisted on moving the government to Chita. The Revolutionary Military Council was assembled to discuss the defense measures, but defense was impossible since there were neither an enemy nor a declaration of war.

The line of explosions was nearing quickly. On the 6th of January Kharkov was destroyed, on the 8th – Ryazan and Vladimir.

— Damn it! What is to be done? — croaked the chairman of RevMilCo.

Nobody could answer him. Jens Boot and Choog were in no hurry. They were the last to leave the doomed places.

— What is to be done? — asked Choog when they were leaving dead Ryazan.

There was no answer.

Meanwhile the chairman of Polish cabinet m-r Tscheteschewski was speaking to the leaders of political parties represented in the Seim:

— I must relay a highly delightful and absolutely confidential message to you. In September of the last year, we as well as our Romanian allies received an offer from our powerful ally and protector France to destroy Russia that until now remained the only dark spot on our bright European horizon. It goes without saying that we agreed.

In December the French military mission came to our country under the flag of the "Society for propagation of French culture." They have delivered to us twenty-eight missile systems "Centrifuge D'Ivoire Excelsior." These missiles were invented in 1928 by French engineer m-r D'Ivoire and were named in his honor. All the works on them were kept in absolute secrecy, and last year the military tribunal of Dijon sentenced one worker to death by firing squad for bragging about his plant that was making some unusual round cannons. The transportation of those missiles was also made clandestinely. On December 28 the installation of those centrifuges was completed in different areas of our country as well as in Romania. On January 1 at 1:00 AM we have commenced our work.

You may easily understand the reasons that do not allow me to go into the technical specifications of these projectile devices.

So, on January 1 we have commenced with the execution of our plan and I can now give you the delightful news: gentlemen, Moscow, Petersburg, Kiev, and other rapists nests are no more! Russia is destroyed.

All the leaders of patriotic parties of the Seim wept with delight and sang "Jeszcze Polska Nie Zginęła" thrice.

Meanwhile former floor waxer Choog staggered across the rubble that was left of the buildings of Ryazan instead of waxing the floors and kept asking Jens Boot:

— What is to be done?

Suddenly he saw something strange that looked like a huge cast iron lentil.

— What is it? — he asked and looked at Jens Boot visibly puzzled.

"D. E. Trust Co." director was a smart man and after examining the lentil thoroughly said:

— This is an unexploded shell. Things like that have destroyed Moscow.

This stirred a lot of interest in Choog and he spent no less than an hour exploring it. There was nothing to explore, to tell the truth, except the "D.E." brand that showed that the shell was made for the "D'Ivoire Excelsior" centrifuge.

— "D.E." — what does it mean? — Choog inquired.

As the readers of the history of "D. E. Trust company" may easily understand those letters could mean many things, and Jens Boot just smirked.

Choog had to decipher those strange initials himself and by doing that he would identify the insidious enemy. And he did it, that ingenious floor waxer who so gallantly had beaten up both French and Polish troops.

— Do you know what it says? — he shouted — D.E. means Dayosh Yevropu.

— Bravo! — replied Jens Boot with utter delight. — Bingo!

But Choog had no use for French compliments. He ran and yelled:

— Comrades, come on, turn the wheel! Let's go and beat them motherfuckers!.. Dayosh Yevropu!..

The director of "D. E. Trust Co." Jens Boot followed him and shouted with his high voice like a young rooster:

— Dayosh Yevropu!

The refugees stopped, blinked for a minute with some hesitation and then turned west. By the evening no less than three hundred thousand men marched to face an invisible enemy. The rumor about that march reached Volga. Millions have joined it from there. People were coming from the north and from the south. On January 6 Sovnarkom declared war. The enemy was still unknown, the decree just said vaguely that the war was conducted against imperialist predators. But all Russia that was rushing to the west as gigantic avalanche knew very well who the enemy was and all Russia marching through the ruins of the cities that were already covered with January snow yelled:

— Hey! Hey! Dayosh Yevropu!..

The Red army marched and elementary school students marched along. Bespectacled Marxists marched and theatrical troupes did. Women, old people, children — all marched west. The Red army soldiers had the machine guns, some peasants armed themselves with old rifles. The majority was armed with clubs. That uncanny army was up to twenty-eight million strong.

Poles and Romanians weren't complacent. Airplanes bombed the hordes day and night. The centrifuges were working non-stop. Poison gases were used. Of the twenty-eight million more than half, sixteen million have perished before reaching the borders of the Republic. But those who survived marched on and no centrifuges could have stopped them.

Choog and Jens Boot marched ahead of everyone and yelled:

— Dayosh Yevropu!

They were near Brest-Litovsk already. An old woman shuffled behind everybody and mumbled quietly:

— Dayosh Yevropu!

She has not yet reached the ruins of Moscow.

Jens Boot was in real ecstasy. He had even forgotten about his "Trust co." He yelled "Dayosh Yevropu." It was a battle cry. With millions other mad people, he was going to chase the red fox out of her hole, that beautiful Phoenician, evil Europe, unforgettable M-me Lucie Blancafort, nee Mlle. Flamengo.

— Dayosh Yevropu!

Twelve million people broke through all the cordons. They stormed into Poland and Romania. They destroyed the centrifuges "D'Ivoire Excelsior."

On January 1 Moscow was leveled.

On February 17 Warsaw surrendered.

On February 24 Bucharest had fallen.

On February 26 m-r Felix Brandeveaux was having telephone conversation with military attaché captain Le Base who was in Krakow.

— Russians are getting close to the German wilderness, — reported captain Le Base. — They shout something strange: "Dayosh Yevropu" and fear nothing, do you hear me — absolutely nothing. Twenty-eight centrifuges have perished. They want to traverse the wilderness and storm into France.

Leaving the phone m-r Felix Brandeveaux called for academician De Laine, the best expert in Russian literature.

— How would you translate "Dayosh Yevropu"? — asked m-r Felix Brandeveaux.

— It is untranslatable, — replied the academic. — It is discordant, it is impolite and, above all, it is unpleasant in the extreme. I wish you never hear these words, my dear prime minister.

— M-r Felix Brandeveaux felt his heart under the plastron. It was beating in a very peculiar way. It was a lot harder to deal with Russia than with the Chamber of Deputies.

— Please, call the head of the seventh secret department of the defense ministry, — he whispered to his secretary. — Right away! Or... or..

19
Some Face Powder

Jens Boot and Choog were drinking the third bottle of Tokay at the old tavern "Pleasant rendezvous" in Krakow. The wine was of the highest quality but Choog was tearful and missed his dear moonshine.

— Just imagine what we used to make in Tambov...

Jens Boot did not argue. Jens Boot was joyful and in good humor. He smiled at the world like an innocent baby. Director of "D. E. Trust co." turned into a regular Red Army soldier without any reservations, simply and honestly. And it could not happen in any other way. Our protagonist was quite impressionable. Once he got fond of something, be it circus tricks, revolution, or stock market speculation — it made no difference, he would fall in love with it till the very end forgetting about any prudence.

He would never renounce his goal, since that goal was more powerful than him. All paths led to it. And now while waking the medieval haughty slumber of Krakow with a wild yell "Dayosh Yevropu" he was doing the same work that he had been doing a few years ago at his thirty second floor office in a mid-size high-rise building.

(It is not that easy to win a woman. Even Zeus had to turn himself into a bull once.)

Jens Boot who moved with the vanguard of Russian army wanted to win Europe. His heart, the impatient heart of the prince of Monaco was beating in perfect accord with twelve million other hearts. Those were the glorious weeks. And Choog was an excellent comrade. So, was it really worthwhile to argue which one was better: Tokay or moonshine of Tambov?

The friends asked for a fourth bottle. Next morning the vanguard of the gigantic army was ready to march on: into Czechia and German wilderness.

The best restaurants in Paris have closed, since the clients have lost all appetite.

Choog's boots were worn out. He rummaged all the shops in Krakow. There were silk kimonos, area rugs from Bukhara, bohemian crystal glasses. But there was not a pair of boots left in the whole city of Krakow. And to get to Paris and conquer Europe Choog the former floor waxer who used to wax the floors being barefoot needed boots. That was understood by the daughter of a sweet-shop owner panna Jadwiga and she gave Choog her father's boots as a gift: the candy-maker was not about to conquer Europe anyways. That is why panna Jadwiga was sitting with Choog and Jens Boot at the tavern "Pleasant rendezvous." If we haven't mentioned that before, it was just because of understandable modesty, in order not to stir the wrong suspicions in our readers.

Choog did not care for women. Choog only cared for the boots and for Europe. It was warm and cozy at the tavern "Pleasant rendezvous." The hostess lit the lamp. Jens Boot looked at Choog and laughed:

— Oh, you really got after real Europeans, didn't you? Powdered your face? Why, all Polish ladies will get crazy looking at you...

Even though Choog finished two out of four bottles all by himself, he somehow understood all the incongruity of those words and came to the mirror that was hanging on the wall next to the picture of the late prime minister m-r Tscheteschewski.

What he saw in the mirror puzzled him even more: strange face covered with flour was looking at him instead of familiar just like his own name ruddy pox-marked mug. Choog wiped his face with his sleeve but nothing has changed.

— Some powder! — he uttered completely perplexed.

Jens Boot took the lamp off the table and brought it closer to Choog's face. He looked for a minute, then put the lamp back on the table and broke into tears.

Jens Boot realized what kind of powder it was. He was crying being seized by hate.

We must now say some words in defense of that long departed and unjustly slandered man.

There is no evil in the world that has not been attributed to Jens Boot. Even now in some North African towns where some lucky Europeans have settled after the destruction of Europe old women like to scare their rowdy grandchildren:

— Just wait, Jens Boot will come and eat you.

Jens Boot had never eaten children. Jens Boot had not committed many other atrocities. Jens Boot had merely suggested that feeble Europeans should do something that they would have done in a hundred years even without his hint. He just had shortened the death throes of Europe. He wasn't the one who invented "D'Ivoire Excelsior" centrifuges. He had only unsealed the rooms of the madhouse. The rest was done by its mad inhabitants. Europeans had invented themselves the most sophisticated ways to exterminate each other.

Jens Boot was neither the author, nor the director of the tragedy that had unraveled in the years 1928–1940. He was merely a stage manager.

Jens Boot was crying out of hate when he saw Choog's powdered face. Although he was not complicit with that atrocity, he was smart enough and experienced enough to realize the horror of it.

— We have to avenge this powder, — he uttered.

Choog was still smiling perplexedly and tried to groom himself in front of the mirror.

After uttering those words Jens Boot suddenly remembered about "D. E. Trust Co." He realized that the bet had been lost and those twelve million people would not conquer Europe. The only thing that was left was precise calculation.

Another two to three years of work. He will get his revenge. He will conquer Europe.

And Jens Boot wiped his eyes and said tersely addressing Choog:

— Farewell.

But Choog still could not understand anything. He just thought that Jens Boot had gotten drunk on Tokay and mumbled:

— So, you are leaving? Okay. Have you paid the hostess for the wine?

Jens Boot went out into a dark square and began to contemplate the quickest escape plan. He did not fear death after Berlin and Moscow. But no time was to be lost.

Jens Boot walked to main street.

It looked unusually lively: there were Red Army soldiers, women from Ryazan in babushkas, workers with harmonicas, nice looking Polish girls, Tatars of Kazan in their bright caps, Polish artists with shoulder length curls, tsadiks with sidelocks.

It was the first evening of the spring, the air was filled with bitter-sweet aroma of poplars.

Russians were supposed to march on next morning. Short sad sounds of the last kisses were heard in the dark side alleys: people who came from the East with the yell "Dayosh Yevropu!" have not yet reached Paris but have already conquered the hearts of many beautiful women of Krakow.

Somebody was playing harmonica. It was a very nice evening.

But confused murmur has spread over the whole crowd when the golden swarm of electric lights went on. All the strollers looked anxiously at the faces of their girlfriends, companions, comrades, and passer-byes. What a horrible carnival: a hundred thousand Pieros wearing white masks.

— I am scared, Galya. You are as white as death!

In mere five minutes the main street was empty. Scared people were trying to hide themselves in the dark alleys and yards, away from light.

Jens Boot walked alone across the field. He walked to the north, to the sea. His calculations told him that it was the only possible way. He suddenly stopped and shuddered: some monstrous thought sprang up in his head. This thought was the simplest one, however: Jens Boot took a small looking glass out of his pocket and examined himself. There was no usual ruddy wind-worn face. What was there looked like a plaster oval.

— I am dying, — Jens Boot thought to himself. — What will happen with the "Trust Co."? Oh, who cares...

He yawned sweetly and went on.

He walked till the dawn, and after the sunrise he sat on a stump, ate a biscuit that he found in his pocket and looked in the pocket mirror again: even dying has not reduced his curiosity. What he saw was his familiar ruddy wind-worn mug that was smiling coquettishly.

(Sometimes even experienced people could be mistaken: when Jens Boot looked in the mirror at night, he forgot about a huge greenish full moon that was shining from above.)

And in Krakow the morning brought no relief. Taking their clothes off people saw that their whole bodies have turned white as if dusted with lime.

Their eyes were sore and tearing. The mouths were dry and sore. The skin of their faces began to peel off and hung in tatters. Horrified people stormed the doctors' offices but no doctor could diagnose the illness. Just one old physician's assistant mumbled significantly:

— The eastern plague. Like the scripture says...

But that philosophical remark was no substitute for a medicine.

By the evening people felt like their skin was burning and their swollen faces suddenly turned red. People were raving with fever. They could not open their festering eyes. People we going blind.

Naked Choog was lying on the floor at the "Pleasant rendezvous" tavern. He pulled of his shirt that felt like cast iron crushing his body. His red swollen body looked like a carcass at a butcher's shop. He was suffocating and even then still whispered:

— Dayosh... dayosh... dayosh Yevropu!..

Blind panna Jadwiga laid next to him. What a strange place the late Europe was!

The girl had managed to fall in love with Choog and now in her last minutes tried to kiss his rotting bloodied hand.

— You are beautiful, pan Choog!..

There was no air. With the last effort Choog croaked:

— Some sort of powder!

And died. It was in the dawn. On March 3 twenty-eight thousand people died of unknown illness in Krakow, seventeen thousand Russians and eleven thousand locals. On March 4 the number of victims has almost doubled.

Russian army did not march on.

Paris was in festive mood. Clerical newspaper "Echo de Paris" wrote:

— God has saved France, the favorite daughter of Apostolic Church.

The freethinking "Ere Nouvelle" gave a different interpretation of the events:

— Even Nature took the side of the Beacon of culture and motherland of Great Revolution"

The readers of both papers felt like their appetite came back. The restaurants have reopened. Parisians were dancing the new fashionable dance "choy" imported from Bolivia.

Jens Boot walked north. Reaching Lodz, he felt that horribly familiar stench of rotting flesh. He did not enter the city. He avoided entering villages and if he saw a man afar he turned aside. He definitely didn't want that strange powder.

However, he had to enter a dead city once more.

The streets of Danzig were strewn with corpses. People who were afflicted with the unknown illness were dying in agony, they were suffocating and therefore crawled out in the streets out of the stuffy air of their rooms. There were no healthy people left, those that were still alive ran away from the city and roamed the woods avoiding each other. But the strongest ones were still coping against doom. Blind people oozing pus crawled among the corpses and licked the drops of rain water off the pavements with their blue tongues suffering from terrible thirst.

Jens Boot found a small boat in one of the warehouses at the port. He pushed it off the shore with an oar, recall Choog's white face at "Pleasant rendezvous tavern" once again and shouted:

— I shall conquer her!

That was on April 1, 1931.

The epidemic of the unknown illness spread quickly. The primary foci were in Poland and Romania. In the next two months those countries were empty. The Russian army that marched victoriously into Europe was destroyed. The remnants of it ran back home spreading the contagion.

At the end of April some sporadic cases of illness were registered in Kazan and Voronezh. The epidemic acquired a mass scale despite of the vigorous quarantine measures and it became an impossible task to save the European part of Russia that has been already devastated by "D'Ivoire Excelsior" centrifuges and depopulated after the march to Europe!.

But the illness has engulfed the southern countries just as quickly. Czechoslovakia, Austria, Hungary, and all Balkan states perished. The epidemic has reached Constantinople. Jemal-pasha ordered to shoot everyone who tried to cross the Bosphorus and by doing that he saved Anatolia.

On July 7 the conference of Western European state assembled in Geneva to discuss the measures to fight epidemic. It was decided to establish a sanitary cordon along the line Bremen — Cologne — Rhine (the western border of German wilderness) and then along the state borders of Switzerland and Italy. Any attempts of the refugees from the afflicted countries to near that line would be stopped by fire and poison gas.

— This is a natural catastrophe. But Europe will be saved, — said m-r Felix Brandeveaux at the conference protocol signing ceremony.

English pilot John Bell undertook a daring expedition to the plagued countries without landing there, of course. He shot a film of dying Vienna from the height of two thousand meters.

The film was great success. Seeing luxurious Ring strewn with corpses sentimental Parisian women wept and powdered their tear-stained faces with fashionable powder "Les Prete."

38th Medical Congress met in Paris. Professor Brieux presented an article about the unknown illness that wiped out Eastern and Southeastern Europe.

— Unfortunately, we have only limited data and could not trace the natural course of that illness. I consider it to be a new yet unknown form of leprosy that unravels with fulminant speed. The incubation period lasts for no more than 48 hours. The immediate cause of death is respiratory failure due to the inflammation of the airways and other mucous membranes. We may only suppose that the illness was brought by the Russians from the East, perhaps from Mongolia and has mutated and spread widely under the influence of European climate. The microbe that caused it has not been identified yet but science moves forward by leaps and bounds. At any rate, I suggest it is named "fulminant leprosy."

That suggestion was accepted. But professor Brieux was wrong: the microbe of the illness was very well known, and to no one else than himself — m-r Brieux worked at the seventh secret department of the defense ministry where he had been cultivating the microbes of plain leprosy until he bred the brilliant strain that has stopped the advance of Russian army.

M-r Brieux, the head of the seventh secret department and sixty pilots that had deployed the test tubes were awarded Legion d'honneur medals.

The last inhabitant of Ekaterinburg died in November, 1931.

Sovnarkom has moved to Chita.

M-r Felix Brandeveaux was trying on Napoleon's hat, that was kept at the Musee Carnavalet until then.

Jens Boot was at London's post office sending a business cable to Mr. Jabbs.

20
On Perniciousness
of European Climate

M-r Brieux was correct when he said that science goes forward by leaps and bounds. In 1932 Swedish scientist Ridelling has identified the microbe of fulminant leprosy and discovered the means to prevent that terrible illness.

Mr. Ridelling's work was not just of theoretical value. No, two people used it to immunize themselves with anti-leprous serum. Those people were Mr. Hardyle and his bride Miss Cate who were getting ready for their honeymoon trip to Central European wilderness.

The wedding ceremony took place on May 12, 1932 at 10:00 AM. The newlyweds went to the air field directly from the church, and the comfortable airplane "Whale" was already waiting for them there.

It was a beautiful day. Blue ocean was shining below. The airplane's cockpit had all the amenities of a steamer's cabin or the sleeper car compartment. But Miss Cate fell ill with air-sickness with all the inconveniences of a seasickness. Mr. Hardyle had to constrain himself with filming clouds speeding past them. But he was a patient man: if he was able to postpone his marriage for five years just to get a good honeymoon trip, he could certainly easily postpone some nuptial formalities for one day.

The ocean shone blue. The clouds rushed on. Cate was chewing on a lemon. Then the moon rose, yellow like Cate's lemon. Next morning they saw the sleepy beauty named

Europe. It looked pale and languid, just as Miss Cate. Mr. Hardyle took a notebook out his briefcase and started a diary considering all the importance of his trip.

This notebook has survived and by showing it to our readers we want to demonstrate a perfect example of heroic inquisitiveness of one middle-aged American. Besides, Mr. Hardyle's diary gives another proof of the noxiousness of European climate.

Mr. W. Hardyle's journey to the Central European Wilderness

11:00 AM, May 13. Flew over the countries that are still alive. Paris looks quite provincial from above. Cate still has not recovered from airsickness. Marriage has somewhat disturbed the regular flow of my thoughts. But I think that it will get back to normal after the first procedures. Hopefully we shall find some shady tree in the European wilderness. I shall be able to think logically once again then.

2:00 PM, same day. We are flying over the wilderness. Ruined cities. Many bones. Northeastern is blowing. Saw an empty city — Nuremberg. Took pictures. Cate thought that the church bells were tolling. But that was an acoustic illusion (due to thin air). I spotted many shady trees. Cate still feeds on lemons.

5:00 PM, same day. We have finally landed. There is real wilderness all around us. I am not afraid at all. 16 degrees eastern longitude, 43 degrees northern latitude. No trees around. We'll have to wait. Decided to take a walk. Cate wants to find European flowers that are named "forget-me-nots," if I am not mistaken, and I want to find a shady tree, doesn't matter which one, I am not so good with botany, I just don't want prickly leaves falling from above.

8:00 PM, same evening. Strange customs! I think that Africa was safer a hundred years ago. But the dangers are quite exciting. But back to our narrative. Took a walk. Some big river. It seems like it was called "the Danube." Cate was looking for forget-me-nots. But we have found only four skulls and a small basin, apparently Europeans used to eat soup out of it. I took it for the ethnographic museum. We then walked to a small house. There were no people inside. Cate said that she would gladly have lived there all her life. I certainly could not agree with her but quickly realized that such a primitive structure with all its originality may serve as a substitute for a shady tree that was nowhere to be seen. There was no furniture in the house. There was a painting on the wall depicting two apples. There were no people in that picture, and the apples looked like natural fruit. I wouldn't have paid any attention to it, but Cate tenderly whispered:

— It's beautiful! Let's take it!.

I must admit that this capricious and expansive temper of my young spouse makes me somewhat scared. But I hope that it will pass after the aforementioned procedures and some sports activities.

I began to unbutton Cate's coat. It was strange, but she paid no attention to me and just kept eating canned pineapple that we took in quantity with us.

Suddenly we have heard a sound not unlike a roar of wild animal. I realized that I was in the wilderness and not at home and ran outside being well armed. Cate followed me still eating a pineapple.

We saw a strange creature that looked like a large ape. But the creature's muzzle was decorated with pince nez glasses, and I realized that it was a man. He was completely naked, and I asked Cate who has not yet become my de facto spouse to look the other way. Considering that a man however naked but using pince nez must be literate I showed him my document where it was written in all different languages that that was a passport of US citizen. But the naked man looked at the can with pineapple and paid no attention to the passport.

With a wild shriek he leapt at Cate and snatched a snack out of her hands, lied on the ground and began to swallow the contents of the can greedily. I could not allow such mischief and tried to teach him with the toe of my shoe. Instead of being shamed of his conduct he bit me in the calf. I then used my gun and the carcass of that wild creature fell into the Danube.

Cate was weeping. I tried to calm her down and told her that my wound was just a scratch, but she uttered then:

— I pity that man. Why haven't you left him alone and let him finish that can in peace?

Yes, Cate's temper worries me more and more, a lot more than my little wound that will heal in a couple of days!

Of course, all the nuptial procedures were out of question after such an accident and we went back to our airplane.

7:00 PM, May 14. Very eventful day; I would say it was a discovery of the traces of ancient civilization. We were walking. Suddenly I saw a lone small house. You can imagine how much surprised I was when I saw a familiar sign at the door that said: "Barber."

I have walked in proudly trying to conceal my emotions. I saw all the signs of normal civilized barbershop. I simply sat in a chair, tilted my head back and waited.

I would allow myself a little philosophical digression now. Although the known procedures are still ahead and I am still somewhat absentminded, I would like to record my thought about barbershops in general. It is such a timeless and space-less institution! In Argentina, in Australia, in Japan you find the same chair and the same mirror. There is something epic and grandiose in that gesture — to sit down, tilt your head back, squint and give you cheeks to the caresses of gentle froth while thinking of eternity!

So, I sat in the chair, closed my eyes, and waited. I was thinking of the transience of earthly matters and of spiritual immortality. I also imagined those different shady trees that I have seen from above.

I came to feeling the gentle touch of a razor. Oh, it wasn't a dream! I was being shaved by a regular barber who entertained me with the latest news, like all barbers in the world:

— First client in three years. Tilt your head back a bit more, please. Some people pass this place every now and then but they grew beards and do not shave. Those are the shortcomings of primitive life. We do get by somehow.

I have managed to get a lot of gunpowder from Vienna at the time of the epidemic. I shoot goats and hares. Our lives are quite miserable though. A wolf has devoured my niece yesterday. Would you care for some cologne?

Old stock. Great pleasure to talk with civilized man. I am the last representative of Europe here. I still keep the door sign and my trousers like a dear relic.

Still absorbed in my thought, I told him:

— Change the door sign. Put "Barbershop of the Universe." It sounds quite original and philosophical.

I gave him a dollar but he refused and asked for a can of pineapple instead.

Suddenly I realized that Cate has disappeared. She was still there when I sat in a barber's chair.

— Cate, — I called her, being quite disturbed.

Then my young spouse emerged from the bushes. Her hair was disheveled by the wind. Noticing her healthy looking flushed cheeks I blessed the beneficial influence of European climate. After the shaving I resumed my search for a shady tree with doubled energy, but Cate said that she was tired and went to sleep immediately, and now I am guarding her innocent sleep so she won't be eaten by wolves like poor niece of the last civilized representative of Europe.

9:00, May 15. My Waterman fountain pen is shaking, although I am on a firm soil. I want to howl like the wild people who roam this wilderness, not write a diary after all things that have happened today. Only the sense of responsibility to mankind forces me to put myself together and describe the events of that terrible day.

I have not slept well last night, the yells of wild creatures kept me awake, also the fact that Cate was so close to me but due to the presence of our pilot she refused to take a cockpit of our airplane for a shady tree. It was a short and very sad night.

After waking up Cate demanded that I go back to the barbershop that I wrote about yesterday. I tried to suggest another route to the places that we have not explored yet telling her that I can shave myself with a safety razor in the cockpit.

But Cate insisted. To my question why we have to go to the place that we already saw yesterday Cate replied that there are European flowers blooming there called forget-me-nots, if I am not mistaken, that she wanted to pick them very much. I agreed, since I didn't want to irritate my delicate spouse before the procedures.

Woe is me! Why have I obeyed Cate? Now I shall never have neither procedures, nor the spouse!

So, I was having a shave and Cate was picking up the forget-me-nots. I was done with shaving, but Cate was nowhere to be found. I called her. Nobody answered. Then I had my head shaved as well to a great delight of the last barber of Central Europe who was rewarded with two cans of pineapple. I had my head shaven although I didn't plan to do that for the fear of wind and common cold. Cate was still missing. I grew extremely worried: she could have been eaten by wolves or even by people. Just remember that one of those horrible creatures had bitten me in the calf. Poor Cate! What happened to her? I was weeping in the barber's chair. The stonehearted barber who was obviously used to these kinds of incidents was just pouring hair tonic on my naked head.

At last, I lost my patience and went looking for Cate. I haven't found any European flowers called forget-me-nots, if I am not mistaken, but I saw Cate. Oh, if only I haven't seen her! Oh, if only she was eaten by wolves or even by people!

Cate was lying on the grass and a naked aborigine with a wooly face wearing a vest was lying on top of her.

— Cate! — I shouted

Neither she nor the human beast has heard my quite loud cry, so much absorbed in their affair.

Alas! I had no more doubts left that they were engaged in the same activity that I wanted to be engaged with Cate under a shady tree. There were no trees there and the midday sun was burning their bodies mercilessly. I am really ashamed to put this scene in my notebook with my Waterman fountain pen. Cate dashed aside seeing me. The human beast got up. He looked like an emaciated ape. Cate hid behind his back. I tried to reason with her. I reminded her of the pastor's words and the laws of our fatherland, but that poor woman who forgot herself just wept and clutched to that wild creature.

Realizing that the human beast wasn't strong or armed I shot him. I was perturbed and could not aim well and wounded him in the leg. The wounded creature was silent. Cate was weeping.

I called the barber. I told him that Cate belongs to me according to the laws of all civilized countries and asked him to help me to take my spouse to the airplane. Clever barber tried to shirk the task telling me that all laws are null and void in the wilderness. He demanded twenty-five cans of pineapple. I had to consent.

We took Cate under the arms. She did not resist but kept weeping. When my poor spouse was in the airplane's cabin I resolved to talk to her.

— Cate! What have you done, Cate?

But Cate broke into a stream of passionate and incoherent phrases. I have recorded some of them that I had memorized:

— I love him, William!.. Please, be magnanimous, let me go to him!.. I want to stay in the wilderness... I now know what love is... It's like air... I was suffocating in America... Do you know anything about the stars?.. You only have oil and curiosity... He was a poet... He lived in Vienna... He read me poems:

My love — what a horror, when poet is in love,

A vagabond God falls in love...

He is beautiful!.. I won't leave!.. Do you hear me, William, I shall never leave Europe!...

After hearing such words, I realized that my young spouse got mentally ill. Mr. Ridelling vaccine has saved us from leprosy but European climate turned out to be pernicious. The very air here is full of tiniest microbes that cause psychiatric disorders that manifest in the rampant paroxysms of love that have nothing to do with either our legal marriages or the night pleasures of our bachelors. Very ominous illness! Disturbing climate!

Therefore, I cannot condemn Cate. I brought her here myself. She is no criminal, just a sick person. My duty is to take her out of here and bring her back to her parents' home. Our divorce is inevitable, of course, since the moral norms and hygienic considerations make any procedures impossible for me in the future.

I am weeping. I tell to myself: Hardyle, you have discovered the European wilderness to the benefit of mankind. But you bought your success at a very steep price, losing your young spouse that has not become your spouse after all.

Cate lies in the cabin and cries. I am awake. There are stars above me, and the aborigines know something about them! Wild people howl somewhere in the woods. One voice is especially horrible. I begin to discern some words. It seems to me that this is a beast that has stolen Cate's honor and he keeps repeating those senseless and criminal phrases that he calls "poems." Why didn't I kill him? That howl probably keeps poor Cate awake.

I have hung the American flag over the ruins. The Central European wilderness belongs to the USA from now on. Let it be my consolation! I don't know how many stars are in the skies above me. But the flag has as many stars as there are states in our country. Hooray!

Cate is still awake. Tomorrow we are flying back to America.

✳ ✳ ✳

The diary of poor Mr. Hardyle ends here, but his trials and tribulations do not.

The airplane was supposed to take off at 8:00 AM on May 16. Cate made several attempts to escape but Mr. Hardyle and the pilot took guard of her.

Few minutes before take-off a wounded human beast crawled out of the woods. He yelled something to Cate. Mr. Hardyle shot again but missed.

The upset husband did not want to waste any more time and ordered the pilot to take off. The airplane got airborne smoothly. But beautiful Cate opened the cabin's door and cried:

— I am staying with you, my love!

And jumped out.

She was laying dead and the wounded human beast was howling over her dead body. It was impossible to tell whether those were the verses of the last poet of Europe or the roar of the beast.

Mr. Hardyle wiped his eyes, put on his eyeglasses, and looked down inquisitively.

America took a lot from dying Europe in those years: gold and statues, singers, and scientists. But on that memorable day it paid a hefty tribute to the dead continent that could only love and howl the most incongruous verses while being in love: the king of oil Mr. Hardyle's young spouse became Europe's trophy forever.

Mr. Hardyle mourned his spouse. But he did not regret for a minute the fact that five years ago he took the offer of Jens Boot. The honeymoon trip was a failure. The continent with such pernicious climate must be destroyed. Seven billion dollars will save lives of many Cates.

As the readers already know the king of oil son was no miser. He loved the mankind sincerely.

21
Total Upheaval in Ethnography

Perished Europeans had a liking for paradoxes: "Rome was saved by geese," "Moscow had burned down of a spark" etc. We are not about to emulate these light-minded philosophers but we have to admit that some seemingly inconsequential events lead to the other ones of profoundly consequential character quite often.

(It is enough to recall prince of Monaco's absentmindedness and its colossal consequences.)

Great Britain was a powerful state. It once possessed the countries that later turned into great powers of our planet, such as: India, Canada, Egypt, Australia and many more. Even in 1930 Great Britain rivaled the USA.

In February, 1930 about a month before the demise of Eastern Europe that was described in preceding chapters, thousands of mailmen delivering the morning mail had tens of thousands similar yellow envelopes with a penny stamp among other letters in their bags.

Those yellow envelopes contained the circulars of "English Steel Trust Co." and were distributed among both retail and wholesale merchants all over the world.

ENGLISH STEEL TRUST Co.
London, date post. Stamp
Gentlemen,
The present is to inform you that due to the public wishes and in order to expand our highly esteemed clientele we have

decided to reduce the prices of our entire merchandise stock by fifty per cent effective March 1 this year.

We dare to express our confidence that you will continue to honor us with your orders.

Well, if geese had indeed saved Rome and venerable Moscow had burned down of a spark, then powerful Great Britain that ruled over four hundred and fifty million people had perished because of those yellow envelopes with penny stamps.

Everything that immediately followed the distribution of that historic circular had no ominous connotations at all. The price reduction of steel merchandize was met by public with affability bordering on enthusiasm. The steel plants of the Trust Co. have tripled their output. Unemployment has ceased to exist. The Trust Co. competitors directors of "Phoenix Steel Co." and the owners of "Bray & Co." wistfully looked at the windows where the insidious adversaries were lurking, where the skies were covered with soot and where the perfect gentle-man God Almighty resided and decided to reduce prices and increase the output as well.

Mr. Hobbes wrote in the "Economics Herald": "An absolute-ly unprecedented flourishment of our steel industry apparent-ly is of an artificial character and fraught with perilous con-sequences." But nobody paid any attention at Mr. Hobbes. He was a man with bad liver doomed to stick to strict diet devoid of soy beans and pickles and therefore completely incapable of adequate perception of any positive events.

Esteemed Mr. Jabbs was indignant when he read the issue of "Pittsburgh News" that reported on the price reduction on steel products in England.

— Of course, Germany is destroyed, but Germany isn't Eu-rope. They will corner all the markets! Rails for Balkan rail-roads. That's one thing. Knives and scythes for Russia — that's two. It's not even worth counting. What is Jens Boot doing? This fool has wiped out poor Germans and became compla-cent. Where are my seven billion? Fraud! Thieves! Hrrrr!

Mr. Jabbs' indignation was expressed in sounds that didn't exist in any human language. His indignation would have

probably doubled should he find out that Jens Boot was buying controlling stake of "English Steel Trust Co." through
some stooges, that he took an active part in this company
management and that that notorious circular announcing the
fifty per cent price reduction had indelible traces of his brilliant penmanship.

The ensuing events, however, have shown that those penmanship exercises of Jens Boot were honestly serving the in-
terests of myopic Mr. Jabbs.

The surplus of the steel goods due to their overproduction
has shown up with perfect clarity. Domestic market was satu-
rated to the brim. American Congress adopted a law that prohibited importation of steel goods. On the other hand, Eastern Europe that used to be the main importer of English steel
goods after the destruction of Germany has turned into gigantic graveyard surrounded by sanitary cordon by the summer of
1930.

"English Steel Trust Co.," "Phoenix Steel Co." and "Bray &
Co." found themselves in dire straits.

By August 1 there were registered one million and six hundred thousand unemployed steel workers. The remaining ones
worked only three days a week.

The steel crisis, the American protective tariffs and the destruction of Eastern European markets have resonated in other
industries as well. The coal harvesting has dropped by thirty-
six per cent. The textile factories were shutting down one by
one. By the end of the year Great Britain was engulfed in unprecedented industrial crisis. Of the workforce that was eight
million and four hundred thousand strong six million and two
hundred thousand were unemployed.

The enterprises went bust. Scores of banks that were con-
nected to industries went bankrupt. English Central Bank ex-
panded credits in order to avert the catastrophe. The machin-
ery of the factories, plants and shipyards was idle. But the
printing presses that issued money were working overtime.
One dollar traded for four hundred and seventy British pounds
at the New York Stock Exchange.

All the buzzards of the transatlantic world have roosted in London. One could easily identify them while they strolled at Picadilly by their trademark plaid pants and ruddy gorged mugs. Due to the wild rise in prices the show of a ruddy well-nourished face in the streets of London's East end where poor people lived became such a rarity that the inhabitants looked around searching for a movie camera when they have spotted one. Those unfortunates took such person for an actor in American movie wearing makeup.

The luxury boutiques and salons were frequented by lazy Argentinians who bought the entire stock of the shops for a handful of pesos — from the cozy underpants made of merino wool to the painting of Rossetti that depicted some nice-looking albeit anemic persons.

Most of the British Museum treasures were acquired by the USA.

Leeds was looted by the crowd of unemployed people.

The conference of British Labour Party came to a conclusion after long debates that the only way to rescue the country was creation of proletarian government.

But the conference has also condemned the "Asian ways of power grab" and adopted a resolution: wait till the Parliamentary election that was scheduled to happen in a year and a half, that is in November, 1933.

At the House of Commons distinguished MP Mr. Chuckane asked another distinguished MP Mr. Broward:

— Is Mr. Broward aware of the fact that one barber named Manuel Braganz that has arrived from Rio-de-Janeiro seven weeks ago has acquired a title of lord for sixty milreis and now sits in the House of Lords?

— No, I am not aware of that, — Mr. Broward replied.

— Is Mr. Broward aware of the fact that in the month of May eleven thousand and for hundred people in Manchester have starved to death?

— No, I am not aware of that either, — Mr. Broward repeated.

— Is Mr. Broward aware of the fact that one continental power is preparing hastily the destruction of our navy?

— Unfortunately, for quite understandable reasons I have no means to answer the question of esteemed Mr. Chuckane at present time.

The newspapers reported that the last session of the House of Commons was of a sluggish character. Nobody was buying the newspapers though — they were too expensive: five pounds for a small sheet of yellow wrapping paper.

However, on July 18, 1932 many have opened their purses and bought the newspapers that contained quite an important announcement: the conference of the representatives from Canada, Australia, New Zealand, India, and other countries of British Commonwealth have decided to sever all the ties with England and declare themselves independent states.

On that day there was a small battle in Liverpool near the city's bakery. Six hundred and fourteen people were killed.

The American charity delegation has arrived at London. Americans have selected twenty thousand children that showed eighty-eight per cent chances of imminent death of starvation on medical exam. They have rejected little Joe, the son of widowed Anne Ice: his chances of dying were estimated at eighty-six per cent.

Anne Ice pled with them to take Joe:

— I swear that he is going to die!

Anne Ice was led out.

Despite all the tragic consequences of the "English Steel Trust Co." circular life in London retained some veneer of normalcy. English conservatism was invincible.

The royal palace was still guarded by the guards wearing powdered wigs, the speakers of Hyde Park were arguing the advantages of anarchy in a dignified manner and frail spinsters cast their faded eyes down while passing the bridges decorated with naked bronze fauns.

Besides, the rough manners were somewhat mollified by the peculiarities of English language: a man who strangled another man for a pound of bread still addressed him using second person plural pronoun.

In Newcastle the unemployed broke with the resolution of the Labour Party and seized power without waiting for the election of 1933. The Parliament condemned their actions and His Majesty's Government sent a few reliable army regiments to Newcastle that did away with undisciplined trade union members.

There was some relief in August thank to decent harvest. But Mr. Hobbes who was still alive despite of his bad liver wrote a brilliant article for the "Economics Herald" where he proved that England has bread supply of her own that wouldn't last for more than two months. Fortunately, the "Economics Herald" wasn't published any longer for want of paper.

The hungry riots resumed in October. The city dwellers headed to countryside estates and farms seizing hidden provisions and devouring not yet slaughtered farm animals. The last race stallion was eaten at Ian estate of lord Haig. Lord Charles Haig had only the tail of the stallion left, and he had this family symbol hung in his empty study over the desk.

Sir Edward Carlisle, the owner of the best collection of bull-dogs demanded a platoon of Scottish riflemen to guard his dogs against the invasion of hungry city dwellers. The request was granted. But the riflemen had eaten up all the dogs pretty soon.

The situation grew direr by the day. The last Americans have left taking grandiose luggage with them.

The government was negotiating with Canada a purchase of grain with the last remnants of golden reserve. But Canadians stood firm and stuck to world prices.

Thousands of people were dying of starvation every day. Another sad day came to pass: November 11. Mr. Broward took the dais at the House of Commons.

— I may now answer the questions posed by esteemed Mr. Chuckane five months ago. French fleet has partially sunk our navy this morning seizing the remaining military vessels.

Machinegun fire was heard in London that evening. But it had nothing to do with political struggle. One group of hungry people was shooting at another group of equally hungry people. Then they fell asleep being exhausted.

At night the king called the leader of the Labour Party Mr. Carl to the palace. Mr. Broward was present at the meeting. The king spoke to Mr. Carl while looking at Mr. Broward who, so to speak, sealed the words of the monarch with the dash of his eyelashes.

— We suggest you to take the reins of power in your hands before the election of 1933 considering our greatly beloved motherland's grave situation, — said the king politely.

Mr. Carl thanked the king and declined the offer just as politely. He was quite terse:

— Thank you, but no thank you!

Mr. Carl was a true democrat. He has shown the king what the constitution was.

Those were the most awful weeks. The hunters have shot all the jackdaws. The ports were serenely quiet as if it was a permanent Sunday in England: not a single small sail yacht docked at the shores of the pauperized country.

Dying people tried their best to keep propriety and dignity. Their moans were muffled, their death throes reserved and they have not forgotten to smile at a priest. It was dignified death but death nevertheless, and there was no deliverance.

At the session of the House of Commons the inquisitive MP Mr. Chuckane was about to pose a very important question to the minister but suddenly fell and kicked his feet. The speaker of the House was appalled by MP's conduct and declared the session closed. But Mr. Chuckane was not guilty of misconduct — he had simply died of malnutrition.

Christmas was coming. People recalled the good old times, the merriest holiday, Dickens-like coziness, stuffed turkeys, happy Mary, and Cate chirping by a fireplace.

On Christmas night dense fog had enveloped the entire island. It was a kind of mercy. The fog had concealed the cities, the houses, and the faces of people in the streets. The cities and towns were empty and dead, the houses were dark, the faces were pale.

However, out of old habit people tried to decorate their empty cold rooms and even tried to smile.

Old lord Charles Haig invited his old friends: lord William Jersen and Sir Edward Carlisle.

Lord Charles Haig's castle presented a strange spectacle. Gigantic empty and cold halls. The fog was coming into them through the broken windows. Lord Charles Haig led his guests through those ominous canyons holding a lantern, its yellow light blinked through the clouds of fog like old moon.

Lord Charles Haig lived alone in his castle. His spouse passed away after eating a pot of half-cooked swedes. His daughter Mary survived by eloping to Canada with some cook-aide of one of the steamers. Lord Haig scorned both his wife and daughter — both have desecrated the honour of the ancient clan: swedes have no place in the menu of Ian castle, and cook-aide does not dare to touch the lord's daughter. Old poor lord Haig has kept his dignity, seldom feasted on fowl, and looked at the horses' tails.

(By fowl he meant crows that frequented the empty halls of the castle.)

On Christmas the lord has put his study in order. Thick volumes still held the images of eleven thousand three hundred and twenty-four coats of arms. The lantern's light was glowing with honey upon the bald heads of three aristocrats. The fireplace was joyfully devouring one of the last armchairs. Large horse's tail that once belonged to Grey, the last stallion devoured by a lowly mob was hanging over the table.

There was delicate coziness everywhere, and the hearts of the old men melted by and by. Three slices of bread that some compassionate old lady gave to lord Charles Haig as a present were served on a beautiful old tray. They seemed traditional plum puddings to two lords and one Sir.

Heart-to-heart conversation ensued. It was of retrospective character, of course. Lord Charles Haig was recalling the horse races of yore. He had recalled the names of all late stallions and mares that had won the Derby cup since 1887.

Sir Edward Carlisle pulled out red foulard handkerchief: the delicate images of late bulldogs were standing in his eyes. Where are you, broad-chested Hume? And you, spotted Bob?

The friends of my golden years! Damned riflemen! All I have left is the ring with an image of dog's head — the prize of XXX-IV dog breeding exhibition.

Lord William Jersen who had never owned purebred mares, nor the gifted male dogs, was also touched nevertheless and wiped his blue eyes. He could sympathize with someone's losses. He didn't have to own thing in order to love them. He also didn't need to see the world in order to know it. Rich imagination and exceptional receptivity have determined the life style of the venerable lord. He did not attend the horse races, nor did he breed dogs. He became the vice-president of "English geographic society" and one of the most renowned explorers of the wild lands, although he had never left his home, moreover — his armchair by a fireplace, where that fearless explorer with his Asian robe and knitted slippers on studied all five continents. As a matter of fact, he did travel every once in a while: he had to attend the meetings of "English geographic society" in London. The trip was taken in a sleeper car and lasted for four hours. But the lord took his hunting carbine, a compass, five-day supply of provisions and fresh water, a map of both hemispheres and a bible — just in case.

On that melancholic Christmas night, seeing tears of his old friends, lord William Jensen endeavored to entertain them with the stories of his travels.

— My dear friends, = he said, — I have seen dwarf people in India in Blue mountains. They live in the trees. Superstitious natives fear them. But we the Englishmen certainly don't.

This brief but entertaining story was a success. The bell of the local church tolled joyfully: Christmas has arrived. Three friends ate their slices of bread in the most dignified manner, imagining them being doused with blue light of burning rum. It must be said that that meager repast irritated their appetite tremendously. Mournful air was just about to fill the study again. But indefatigable lord William Jensen encouraged by the success of his first story has resolved to fight it off decisively.

— I have seen many things, my dear friends. I have seen terrible things. The current hardships of our great motherland pale by comparison. Just make your own judgement: at the shores of lake Daish in Central Africa that I have discovered there live real cannibals. I saw with my own eyes a man who ate another man.

— It is horrible indeed, — lord Charles Haig replied. — I hope those criminals weren't English.

— Oh, of course not! They were Negroes, that is black people with black souls.

The story had animated the listeners a great deal. The friends prayed for the wellbeing of His Majesty the king and congratulated each other with the holiday. Lord Charles Haig gave his friends Christmas presents.

— You, my dear lord I present with crystal decanter embossed with my coat of arms and wrapped into a napkin, it can serve you as a flask in your travels to wild lands. And you, my dear Sir I shall present with some modest gift, I want to give you a live and purebred bulldog that was spared from being devoured by mob. Please, go with me. And you, my lord, just have a rest in the meantime. Lord Charles Haig and Sir Edward Carlisle left the study. Thick fog engulfed them. Lord was panting.

— I don't see anything. Where is your dog? — asked Sir Edward.

— The dog is farther down.

They walked down the dark empty halls.

— We have to go down these stairs, — uttered the lord at last.

The steps were slippery. It was dripping from above. A rat squeaked somewhere. They were in the dungeon.

— I am scared my lord. Where is the dog?

— You see, the dog got tired. It lies nearby. Bend over, Sir and you will see it.

But Sir Edward Carlisle did not bend over. Then the real dog's howl was heard. It was lord Charles Haig who was howling, after eating a slice of bread he got an incredible appetite. Sir Edward finally believed in the existence of a bulldog and bent over.

The cracking of the joints and gnashing of teeth was quite audible...

Lord William Jersen was waiting for his friends for a long time. He then resolved to undertake a trip. He picked up a yellow lantern and went to look for his friends. One empty hall looked just like another. Lord got lost. He could not find any people at all. He could not find a habitable room either. The squall of wind blew out the lantern. Lord cried out but his cry was muffled by thick fog. He then lied on a wet floor and wept like a baby.

At long last, the windows have lightened up a bit. It was a lifesaving dawn. Lord William Jersen got up and resumed his search, shuddering. He soon found the door of the study. Opening it he froze with amazement. There was a basin and plates with coat of arms on the table. Lord Charles Haig was wiping his lips with a napkin and pushed the plate aside. The basin was spreading an aroma of a good homemade broth.

— Oh, this is you, my dear lord! I worried about you. Please, share this modest repast with me.

The face of lord Charles Haig quite satisfied with his supper was beaming with joy, serenity, and peace.

— But where is our friend Sir Edward Carlisle? — the great traveler asked sitting at the table.

— He went home with his bulldog.

Lord William Jensen took a spoon. Pale light of December morning was oozing throw the misted window glass. The lord looked in the basin, issued a muffled scream and fell to the floor.

Good host had not even bothered to take the ring with dog's head image off Sir Edward Carlisle's hand.

December 28 was considered to be a regular work day. London lived its usual life. The royal guards still wore their white wigs. Unemployed people were firing machineguns. Starving clerks were dropping dead in the streets. Some oddballs argued about the date the last Englishman would die: pessimists said that it would happen in January, optimists thought that it should happen in May.

But Englishmen were dying with dignity, and life was going on as usual. On the 28th of December a number of meetings took place at various scientific and educational societies, and among them was a meeting of "English geographic society" dedicated to the presentation of the ethnographic research of the African tribes in the upper Nile valley.

The meeting opened at 3:00 PM. The speaker Mr. Howe began with:

— As we know...

But at that moment a strange man stormed into the room with wild eyes, unshaven and looking extremely indecent. The chairman recognized with great difficulty that it was no one else than the vice-president of the society lord William Jersen:

— I have to interrupt the speaker, — wheezed lord William Jersen. — Extremely important announcement! An upheaval in ethnography! Gentlemen!

Lord's voice has died out. He was given a glass of water.

— Gentlemen, attention please! A gentleman has eaten another gentleman!

Hearing that the chairman frowned, then smiled and began to clank his teeth suspiciously. The youngest and the fattest of all society members who grew up on good Dutch milk got up then and ran to the window. The society was located on the second floor, so the cautious man jumped down without injuring himself.

— You are supposed to exit through the door, not through the window, —

the guard said disapprovingly and shook his white wigged head.

— It depends, it depends, —

replied Jens Boot quite rightly, since the resourceful tourist that has grown up on Dutch milk was indefatigable Jens, of course.

22

It's just Bad Peroxide

Dark rumors about some omnipotent Dutchman began to stir the remaining European countries just after the successful English campaign. The beaux at Parisian balls were raving about the "Flying Dutchman."

Serious politicians just mumbled at the bridge parties:

— What's going on in Europe?! England is done for... That's no Van Houten!..

"Le Matin" published an article full of curious hints: "We got reports that great Dutch adventurer Jean Botha, who is the grandson of renowned Boer general, is implicated in the chain of catastrophes that has destroyed three quarters of Europe. He has avenged the offenses committed by England against his grandfather.

According to some data Jean Botha was working at German General Staff and coordinated the attacks on our banks in Berlin at the time of implementation of known sanctions.

Jean Botha is married to a daughter of American billionaire Mr. H. He was one of board members of "English Steel Trust Co."

The Prosecutor's Office is taking measures to find whereabouts of this dangerous subject."

"Le Matin" article was reprinted by the papers all over the world, which intrigued the public even more. The descendants of general Botha sued the editor of "Le Matin" for defamation. American journalists who paid a special visit to Holland had to confine themselves to the description of picturesque national costumes and reports about Rembrandt's painting being stolen, since no traces of that mysterious adventurer were found.

Clerical "L'idee Nacional" was insisting on so called Dutchman to be in fact Russian communist carrying out the program of the XVIII congress of Comintern. Communist paper "Le people," to the contrary, swore that Botha was no one else than m-r. Victor Brandeveaux, prime minister's nephew who has vanished mysteriously and was bound on establishing worldwide monarchic dictatorship.

The beaux did not argue about who was right. Covering their eyes with fans they were waiting to get invited to dance a tour of choy by "The Flying Dutchman." The beaux were good Catholics and believed in miracles.

All Europe was talking about Jean Botha. But the Blancafort couple talked of something totally unrelated in their lofty boudoir at Venetian palazzo. They were talking about shoes.

— Give me six thousand liras. I need to by these grey suede shoes, — Lucie whimpered.

— I have no money, my pussy. I have lost everything on pounds. Franc and lire — both are falling. It's quite likely that we'll be begging for bread crumbs tomorrow, — Jean tried to reason with her.

— I need shoes.

— But you've bought a pair just last week.

— Those were the satin ones, for the balls.

— You have a hundred pairs of shoes, my pussy.

— You're lying, you're lying blatantly! I only have eleven pairs: white satin ones, black ones for the ball, black suede ones, yellow ones for outdoors, black ones for outdoors, red Morocco ones for a masquerade, Brussels ones with pompoms, another yellow one with buckles and modest grey ones that match the stockings. That's all. The rest are boots or low boots. I need the grey suede ones now. Six thousand liras — that's nothing.

— My pussy, I have no money. We are ruined.

— You have squandered it! You've spent everything on your paramours, — yelled Lucie, getting quite mad at him. Her red forelock was shaking.

— My pussy, you know very well that I am no longer capable of that, — Jean babbled humbly trying to avert the scandal.

Pussy knew it better than anyone, but jealousy had all the logic beaten up, and she went on:

— You're lying! Gimme six thousand liras.

— I don't have it. Pounds are worthless. The lire's falling down. Life became impossible. If that damn Dutchman does in Italy tomorrow, we are dead.

— What Dutchman are you talking about?

Jean was glad to switch the topic of their conversation.

— Don't you know, my pussy? All Europe is talking about him, his name is Jean Botha, it seems to me.

Lucie rubbed her forehead under the red lock with her pink fingers. Lucie had beautiful forehead and good memory.

— Jean Botha?.. Wait a minute... Oh, it must be that pig that tried to harass me and then sent me a letter...

Lucie opened her armoire and took out big box full of various souvenirs. There were the letters of her bridegroom and twenty-two paramours, somebody's suspenders, a stack of photographs, a lock of mandolinist and even a moustache of the charming gondolier. Lucie Blancafort led quite a vibrant life for her thirty-six years.

Rummaging through all this trash she found a postcard with pansies. The ink at "Kaffir's smile" tavern was of pretty poor quality. The letters of that meaningful epistle have faded but the signature was still legible: Jens Boot.

— What did he write you, my pussy?

Ever since Jean lost his amorous capacity Lucie has stopped concealing her love affairs from him. That is why she eagerly answered her husband:

— He wrote in a very poetic way. He promised me everything. Not like you, just look at yourself! Can't even give me six thousand liras for suede shoes! Forces me to go barefoot!

— But what did he write?

— He wrote that my single word is enough for him to make me the queen of some country, I think Phoenicia.

— Phoenicia?.. No, that won't do. But maybe he can raise the exchange rate of lire instead. Then we'll live like royals. Try it, my pussy, maybe you can do it.

All women are afflicted with vanity. Lucie, whose abilities were questioned by her husband, naturally agreed. Especially after the beautiful gondolier with his remaining right whisker had disappeared without trace leaving Lucie just his left whisker.

Next day various Italian newspapers printed an announcement:

— Jens, please, come! Make me your Phoenician!

Your Lucie.

After jumping out of the second-floor window just on time Jens Boot immediately went searching for a boat. Reaching Paris and recalling the chairman of "English geographic society" clanking his teeth he felt a shudder and, therefore bought a ticket to Rome.

Jens Boot was quite satisfied with his stay at that very ancient city. First of all, he was able to carry out some tasks of "D. E. Trust Co." including some major colonial operations, and second of all, the Romans were still eating pasta and there was no need to jump out of the upper floor windows.

On one beautiful evening when swallows were circling over Piazza di Spagna and darkened it when flying lower, when the bronze nymphs shed their wanton tears, Jens Boot decided to check the exchange rate of the lire and bought a newspaper. The charms of the spring are great and awesome, indeed! He tried in vain to unfold the newspaper, the eyelashes of a flower girl were too dark, the violets' aroma of mythical lawn and heavenly moss was too strong, it was too much love in a small space of Piazza di Spagna.

Jens Boot sat on the marble steps and went into a dreamlike state. The dying light of the red forelock belonging to divine M-me Lucie Blancafort nee Flamengo was still burning over the round domes and black pines of Rome.

A bunch of violets laid over the unfolded newspaper. Jens Boot was dreaming.

He picked up the newspaper then. Violets fell on the ground. He did not find the exchange rate of the lire. He was running toward the train station yelling wildly and knocking off pedestrians, just like he ran a few years ago together with Choog — the floor waxer across the snowy desert to conquer Europe. Swallows were still flying. The nymphs were still weeping. A train to Venice was departing at 9:20.

Next evening around 8 o'clock Blancafort couple was eating rice with compote. A self-important butler worthy of palazzo that formerly belonged to Marquis Fermuccini handed Lucie a card:

JENS BOOT
Executive Director
D. E. Trust Co.
New York City Europe

See? How about it? — whispered Lucie and shook her fore lock smugly.

— I am leaving, — Jean babbled. — I am going. See you tomorrow. Please, my pussy, try your best. Good night. The main thing is lire, exchange rate. You'll get a hundred pairs of shoes.

But Lucie wasn't listening already.

In half an hour Jens Boot with his coarsened body and embittered soul had entered those mythological realms where gods turned into wild bulls and the bulls acquired divine guises. He was at the heart of Europe.

The swallows were still circling faraway over Rome bringing darkness and love. The bronze nymphs still wept.

It was dark at M-me Lucie Blancafort's boudoir. Faint lantern was hanging lonely and dead, like polar sun. It did not signify anything but the red divine forelock was glowing in blue dusk. Water was dripping somewhere in the bathroom.

(Lucie did not weep. But the nymph's tears kept flowing)

Jens Boot who was used to the heavy smells of ink, printing toner, chemical labs, blood, corpses now smelled spring in

Venice. It began with the sad breath of the canals and ended with coveted forelock that smelled of water lilies and irises.

So, on March 19, 1933 at 8:45 PM Jens Boot went mad. He was dashing across small boudoir back and forth with that incomprehensible trophy on his shoulders, tipping off the blue Venetian glass vases and flasks and yelled:

— I found you, my Phoenician!

After forty years of hard labor, after many trials and sufferings, and disappointments Jens Boot at last has found all the bliss of shared love.

He didn't say anything. Lucie also didn't say a word, only sighed, and moaned with pleasure: Jens Boot was no Jean Blancafort. It would be impossible to count the number of kisses. Polar sun was glimmering detachedly, and pedantic nymph was counting seconds in the bathroom.

In the middle of the night Jens Boot suddenly recalled that he was waiting for Lucie Blancafort nee Flamengo for nineteen years exactly. It has upset him for a moment. Like any plain folks he would like to hear the words of remorse and love from her.

— Lucie, say: "Thank you, I am dancing."

And suffocating under the weight of that incredible feeling and eighty-seven kilos, which was Jens Boot's exact weight, Lucie uttered promptly:

— Yes, yes! Thank you, I am dancing!

What happened next? Catastrophe? Lucie's death? The final demise of Europe?

No, something more awful happened and did not happen at the same time: the simple morning came. White fog oozed through the window blinds and smothered polar sun. "Oranges from Messina, oranges!" was heard in the streets; nymph's tears were not heard anymore. Jens Boot laid on his back with his eyes shut. He was still happy. The idea to send the "Trust Co." to hell, to go to Phoenicia with Lucie, to eat dates there and kiss her crossed his mind. He smiled. Then Lucie dared to talk:

— Mon petit Jean! I love you so much. I shall always dance choy with you. With you only. I was waiting for you — deep inside, without even knowing it myself. Some incredible things are told about you: like you are some sort of a king of Europe. I just want to ask you one little favor: please, make the lire to rise. Just for a week. We need it so much. Please, give me this nice surprise, mon petit Jean! Make it, and I shall kiss you.

Jens Boot still laid on his back with his eyes shut. But he wasn't smiling anymore.

Lucie went on:

— You don't answer me? You don't want to? But this is shocking! We are ruined. I can't afford to buy simple shoes. It's outrageous! Why are you silent? Of course, I love you. But I cannot afford the luxury of the nights like that without surprises. Times have changed. You were satisfied, weren't you?..

Jens Boot opened his eyes then, still contemplating. What he saw was horrible indeed. Jens Boot who saw dead lovers on the balcony in Nuremberg, who saw Choog's powdered face and the scowl of the chairman of "English geographic society" closed his eyes again in horror.

He discovered the greatest fraud in human history: M-me Lucie Blancafort nee Flamengo turned out to be not a Phoenician princess but an aged fat woman that looked like cheap whore of Marseille or Genoa. Sagging breasts and flabby belly spilled over the bed sheet. Powder has partially peeled off the face unmasking furrowed skin pocked with zits. Small eyes were almost lost in the pillows of flab.

Jens Boot felt very depressed. He laid there for a long time not looking at Lucie and not listening to her chastisements. Nineteen years of deception! M-me Lucie Blancafort was not worthy of God's visit.

Suddenly he remembered something and whispered:

— But it can't be... But that forelock... that divine forelock...

Jens Boot opened his eyes again and looked with great anxiety at his last hope, at that gorgeous dawn of hair. But the fate has been obviously sneering at him:

dirty-greenish hair that looked like peatbog's slime was showing through the golden sunset.

— What is it? What is it? — cried Jens.

— I told you already that we are ruined. It's just bad peroxide.

Jens Boot jumped out of bed. He raised the window blinds. There was dead Venice behind the window, rotten canal water, unaired fumes of the rotting houses, abomination, decay, death.

And next to him an aged insolent woman in lacy panties spread the smell of her face powder that tickled his nose, and begged:

— Please, make the lire rise! Mon petit Jean, please, do it!

Jens Boot could not stand it anymore and sneezed so loudly the all the flasks that weren't yet broken at night clinked apologetically.

He left the room then. No, he did not rush to the stock market to raise the falling lire, he just went to the bathroom where the lachrymose nymph was weeping at night. Jens Boot washed his whole body with cold water and damned the night of love.

After that he called the self-important butler, gave him one hundred dollars to be passed to M-me Lucie Blancafort and left the palazzo of former Marquis Fermuccini.

Poor Jens, we can only imagine what he felt sitting in a gondola and listening to the gondolier's songs about immortal love!

At the train station café Jens Boot ordered a bottle of soda and took out his small notebook. It had a small map of Europe in it. He touched the map with a tiny red-and-blue pencil. The beauty's body was already almost rid of people.

"It's March 29, 1933, — he thought. — Very well. Let's move on."

And red-and-blue pencil crossed the head and the right arm of the coveted princess.

23
"I Don't Remember Anything"

Delicate hills of Umbria reminding of young girls' body were seen behind the train car window, and red sunset. Jens Boot tried not to look at the window.

"Damn memory, — he was thinking. — If only I had not remembered anything! If only I could clear my head of all the mythology lessons that I was taught at middle school, and that specter at the "Tea Star": a young girl with fiery red forelock, bad peroxide indeed! If only I could forget love!"

Those were Jens Boot's thoughts. The spring was showing its green splendor behind the window. The train was going to Rome. Jens Boot listened to the knocking of train's wheels, their familiar language that seemed as natural as ticking of "Omega" pocket watch in his vest, like the heartbeat under it — the measure of longitude, the tread of time.

That has consoled him but a tiny bit. He began to listen to his fellow travelers' talk.

— The price of oil has gone up by three hundred liras, — young beautiful woman said mournfully.

— Just wait till Giovanni Botto comes here, you'll see more, — replied someone.

— They say that he is in Rome already and has brought some colossal cannons.

One venerable silver-haired passenger interfered in that conversation:

— It is quite demonstrative of dying civilization! Superstitions flourish. Some grub-street journalist invented that Botto while drinking his mug of beer and — hey, presto! — everybody, just think of it — not just the old hags, no — politicians, writers, even some scientists believed in him.

Jens Boot definitely felt offended hearing deliberations of that venerable passenger. His father was not some grub-street journalist but a potentate of a state, albeit a small one. But he preferred to keep his incognito minding common peoples' spite.

Conversation went on. An elegant sportsmanlike gentleman seconded the opinion of the venerable passenger.

— Yes, everybody became awfully superstitious. Sometimes it seems to me that we are going back to medieval times. You probably have heard a new fable already: that there is an outbreak of a new mysterious illness named ciquita in Brindisi and Naples. I met one well educated man in Bologna, a director of pasta factory who decided to leave everything behind and emigrate to Argentina once he has heard about that ciquita. It's universal madness!

The lady sighed mournfully, opened her basket, took out poppyseed cookies and offered them to other fellow travelers. Jens Boot also got one of the cookies. He was so sensitive to woman's kindness in those tragic hours! Finishing a cooky he looked expressively at his beautiful fellow traveler. But her facial expression was just the one of caring mother. He then decided to talk to that beautiful lady. Beautiful signora Lucia Giorno has really touched his heart with her devotion. Signora Lucia was twenty-two years old and her young years were quite sad despite of her beauty. She married piano tuner Pietro Giorno at the age of eighteen. Everything looked so good to the young newlyweds who loved each other dearly. But a week after their wedding Pietro was mobilized and sent to Tripoli. Pietro was fighting in a war for four years. Lucia was waiting for him for all those four years. She was desperately poor and earned her piece of bread by embroidering the rich ladies' garters. Seven days of bliss and four years of parting — that was her life. But a week ago she received a postcard from Brindisi. Pietro wrote that he got a leave warrant and was coming to

Rome. He would stay at the vacant room of his brother at via Cavour. Lucia embroidered garters for seven days and nights to earn money for the ticket to Rome. But now she was worried: it seemed like via Cavour was quite far from the train station and she didn't even have fifty liras for a tram ticket. And what should she do with a basket?

Jens Boot, although lost his love, could still respect it in the others. He wiped his eyes with a handkerchief being sincerely moved and offered signora Lucia to give her a lift to via Cavour where impatient husband was waiting for his spouse.

The rest of the way Jens Boot spent conversing with the venerable passenger. There are many stories about chance encounters along the way. But Jens Boot was surprised a lot when he learned that the modest gentleman with grey locks that got a poppyseed cooky from Lucia and ate it with pleasure was Francesco Bari — one of the most prominent philosophers of the last decade.

Jens Boot had never been a bookworm, let alone a reader of philosophical treatises, but he had to look through a lot of newspapers daily and he saw that name there quite frequently. The great philosopher had published a book in 1931 "Transience and Essence" in which he had analyzed with great foresight a process of European demise and all conceivable transformations of Europe's existence.

Francesco Bari touched on his favorite topic almost against his will while conversing with Jens Boot. He began to talk about the end of Europe. It wasn't a political review, nor a moral lamentation: the philosopher spoke of life and death, of black seed, green sprout, and gorgeous rose. It seemed like he felt its thick heavy aroma at the tips of his fingers — the midday heat of Florentine Renaissance.

Francesco Bari did not chide anyone and did not argue with anyone. It was just a biography, but biography narrated by a man in love: every birth mark turned into a myth.

A drop of beeswax on the shoulder of sleeping Eros. A stone egg in the blue dusk of a catacomb. A resounding "montjoie" of hairy gloomy men who paved the great roads of Europe with their own bones. A dark tavern where an executioner who just had twisted someone's joints and a pious thief were feasting together — a sudden whisper. Rose of Roses, Daisy of Daisies. Amen. An explosion of light. Save your souls, the world is flooded by the sun! Fullness and austere sadness of a drafting set, where there is a compass and a number, of the rose, of a skull and two bones, of marble, of light. A wild bird of Leonardo. Polite hollowness and tribulations of Candide. A roar of Carmagnola. A wig on a pike. Yellow gunpowder cloud and other theatrical effects of the Corsican. Progress. Comfort. Hollowness but without politeness now. A crutch. And the last leaps. "C'est la lutte finale..." at Pere Lachaise amidst the glass bead wreaths and rusty blood. The finale, however, is different.

Thus spoke Francesco Bari. Jens Boot listened to him being quite moved since he just heard the story of the high and bitter days of his love.

The blossoming and death of Europe merged with his personal misfortune. When Francesco Bari was speaking about the epoch of Lorenzo: "It was like a stop at the zenith of being. Silver reins dropped out of driver's hands. It seemed like the red-maned horses that raised their hooves would never lower them again..." — Jens shuddered. Could it really have happened in XV century in Florence and not in 1914 at the "Tea Star"?

Unforgettable Lucie!

And when Francesco Bari said with a bitter smirk: "And here is the agony. Stupid greed of some Brandeveaux. Nobody speaks about great principles of human rights any longer, even for the sake of ordinary decency. Everything is clear..." — Jens Boot interrupted him with incomprehensible exclamation:

— It's peroxide! It's just bad peroxide!

Jens Boot stayed silent after that. The others were still talking about that fabled ciquita, about Giovanni Botta, about the weather. Jens stayed silent and thought:

"Why can't I forget all that? Why do I have to keep all those tender specters? I want to cry. I don't want to live. Dead Europe. A useless passenger in a dark dirty train."

Finally, they have reached Rome. And Jens Boot for the first time had realized that that city so familiar to him was nothing else but a stone memory, terrible curse of all men.

Those buildings were not just buildings but petrified time. The years did not dissipate in the light ether there but stayed to press the suffocating earth with marble and granite heels. There stood a gigantic skeleton whose every vertebra reminded of Francesco Bari's words.

Evil fate has led Jens Boot who yearned oblivion to no other place but Rome. But there was nothing else to do: the doors of the car opened and Jens though being quite upset went out on a platform, however, not forgetting signora Lucia's basket.

It was a touching parting. Francesco Bari invited Jens to visit him and talk at leisure about the same thing — that is about the strange fate of Europe.

Jens Boot gave signora Lucia a lift to via Cavour as was promised. They were searching for signor Giorno's room in a big seven-story building for a long time. At last, some boy showed them a dark spiral staircase:

— Here, at the very top, third door.

— Signor Giorno? — Jens Boot asked when the door bell was answered by a man with pale emaciated face.

— It's me. How may I help you?

But Lucia pushed Jens aside and dashed toward the door.

— Pietro! It's you! My love!

— I am sorry, you are mistaken.

— Pietro! You don't recognize me! Santa Maria! What's the matter with you?

Jens Boot thought that the darkness caused the confusion and lit a flashlight that he had in his pocket. Bright light enveloped the shaken woman.

— Pietro! Do you see me now? No? Good Lord, are you blind?

— Blind? Porca Madonna! What nonsense! I can see you very well. But you must have knocked on the wrong door. At least, I don't know you.

— What's wrong with you, Pietro? It couldn't be that I have changed so much. Just look at me!

Poor Lucia hugged her spouse, kissed him, and burst into tears.

— Pietro, my boy! Just kiss your poor girl! I have been waiting for you for so long!

Jens Boot turned his flash light off, feeling ashamed.

Pietro grouched:

— What an insolent kind of bimbos we get nowadays. Storm in the rooms just like that...

— Pietro! I'm gonna die! Pietro!

Pietro answered after a minute hesitation:

— You seem to be a nice-looking girl... quite smartish too. Come in, if you really want to. But I am just a soldier on a leave warrant, you won't earn more than five hundred with me.

The door closed. Jens Boot stayed outside with a basket. Recalling the dialogue and sickly emaciated face of Pietro Giorno he began to fathom the meaning of what was going on.

He lit a cigarette and went downstairs slowly leaving a basket at the door. At the bottom of the stair well he heard sounds of a woman crying and rough man's voice upstairs:

— Enough! Take your money and be gone!

A minute later something dashed down the dark stair well. At the bottom of it laid poor Lucia's dead body.

People were asking each other:

— What happened?

— A wench fell down the stair well. Must've been drunk.

— Could it be ciquita perchance?

Everything went quiet after that.

Poor signora Lucia Giorno, she was waiting and embroidering garters for four long years for the sake of that minute!

Jens has guessed many things correctly. He wandered dark streets being in the gloomiest mood. A tram car was speeding on right in front of him. Pale face of the driver looked confused. There were no passengers or conductor on board, they somehow managed to bail out. Only one woman with a baby stood at the rear door and screamed desperately. The tram was rushing on for an hour along the quiet streets, along the empty tracks. It was 2:00 AM, no other trams were running. Rare pedestrians smirked:

— A tram has gone mad.

— Ciquita?

A woman was still screaming. At 3:00 AM the tram jumped and stopped somewhere in the outskirts of the city. The driver got out and yawned absentmindedly: it's late, time to go to sleep. The woman was silent now. The baby was the one who screamed and tried to suck cold dead breast in vain.

Next morning Jens Boot witnessed a strange scene. A properly attired signore with a ribbon in his buttonhole stood at piazza Venezia in downtown Rome. Squinting his myopic eyes at the pedestrians and lifting his bowler hat he asked:

— Excuse me, signore, would you be so kind to tell me where am I and who am I?

Pedestrians were rushing away from him instead of answering and whispered:

— Ciquita! Ciquita!

Piazza was deserted in no time. Two policemen came to see what was the matter but hearing the man's question immediately forgot about their duties and broke into tears.

Jens Boot did not run away from piazza Venezia. He stood next to that properly attired gentleman for a long time. It wasn't compassion that kept him there, no — it was envy.

— If only a had been like him! Lucie... Europe...damned Rome!

Buttercups were blossoming and cats were meowing near Colosseum. Newspaper boy ran toward Jens and yelled:

— Ciqiuta in the Chamber of Deputies!

"Grave incident occurred today during the discussion of the bill concerned with the establishment of consulates at Harbin and Samoum. The esteemed deputy from Napoli signor Ettore Cerapuzzi took the dais, opened his mouth to introduce an amendment but has not uttered a single word. Everybody in the chamber shuddered. Some deputies dashed toward the exit door. The shout "Ciquita" was heard from the visitors' rows. With that all the deputies dashed to the doors tipping over the benches and crushing each other. Deputies from Torino signor Cesare Pligni and from Arcona signor Paolo Valdi have died of inflicted injuries. The Chamber of Deputies has been dissolved."

The streets of Rome resembled the lobby of the Chamber of Deputies on that day. People rushed down the streets like a scared flock of sheep, then stopped abruptly and looked around stupidly being totally confused. Buses and trams rushed off their regular routes colliding with each other. Many shops stayed open all night long. Looting was going rampant.

In the evening gigantic catastrophe happened at Rome Termini station. The dispatcher on duty was rubbing his head in confusion — he forgot the schedule. Express train that ran from Naples to Paris collided with a local train that ran from Rome to Bologna. 814 people were killed. The dispatcher was arrested. He smiled and whistled the tune of choy on his way to jail.

One word only was heard in Rome. In old days they used to say: "pasta with sauce," "kiss me," "how is lire today?" — now everything was forgotten. Pasta could get cold. Naïve lips were waiting for a kiss in vain. Lire was falling but nobody gave a damn.

There was no pasta, neither there were kisses, nor liras. Ciquita was in Rome.

The city medical management office was keeping the record. There were suspicious cases of illness:

Before April 1	8
April 1	23
April 2	311
April 3	619
April 4	2487
April 6	911
April 7	4317
April 8	811

There were no data after that since all the staff of medical management office was afflicted with ciquita on April 8.

Rome's correspondent of "Le Temps" who was able to escape to Nice just in time described the new disease as following:

"Ciquita is undoubtedly a dangerous form of malaria. It was brought by soldiers from Tripoli. A punitive expedition was sent in January of this year to one of the independent oases, namely to Ghat. All male natives were exterminated immediately, females too but later, after serving the needs of the troops. The soldier of 17th infantry regiment fell ill with fever but recovered quickly. But the illness left serious complications: Nicholas Petri lost his memory completely. He could not remember even his own name. There were several similar cases among the 1118 troops who were on leave warrants on board the transport ship "Regina Elena", among those troops were those who took part in the expedition to Ghat. "Regina Elena" has docked in Brindisi on March 12. In a week, that is on March 19 an epidemic was raging in Brindisi. From there it moved to Naples and by the end of March — to Rome.

A person afflicted with ciquita at first experiences high fever (40–40.5C) usually at night. The fever lasts for 4–6 hours. In the morning a patient feels recovered, just somewhat fatigued. He tends to consider the night fever to be just a bad dream. He gets up as usual and even goes to work. But here is the insidious nature of ciquita. Specific toxin produced by its microbe affects the brain cells: a patient loses his memory. Sometimes this loss is complete, in that case a patient does not remember anything and turns into a savage. Sometimes the loss is partial, a patient cannot remember faces or names. A wide variety of partial memory loss has been described: one patient has forgotten all numbers and signs (unfortunately he worked as a dispatcher at the power plant), the other who was a well-known poet Mario Pucci forgot his native Italian language but retained the ability to speak French, etc. The paroxysms of fever recur every 24 hours. Patients usually die of heart failure after 4–6 paroxysms. There were no reports of complete recovery yet.

As for the modes of transmission of ciquita, it is still hard to say something with certainty. But professor of the university of Rome signor Canio made some successful experiments before he died. Signor Canio came to the conclusion that the microbe of ciquita is spread by common fleas. Mosquitoes and other parasites do not carry it. If this hypothesis is true, it is quite understandable why ciquita found such a fertile ground in Italy. In my last Rome report I had already mentioned the massive invasion of fleas at that city..."

Such was the special correspondent's description of ciquita on the pages of "Le Temps." Well, he was earning his bread honestly and his article was not far from truth, by and large. However, it missed one important point: a small patriotic union "D.E." — "Decapitazione degli Ebrei" has not found enough Jews in Italy to cut their heads off and decided to deal with Arabs. Someone by the name of Giulio Cicharetti, the secretary of "D.E." union learned the climate peculiarities of Tripoli very thoroughly. The punitive expedition to Ghat oasis was sent after the loud media campaign and on the insistence of "D.E." union.

Jens Boot was not bragging when he crossed the head and arm of Phoenician princess at the train station café. Just before his sad trip to Venice he had a conversation with Giulio Cicharetti at a modest dairy shop.

— A glass of warm milk, — Giulio asked.

Finishing his milk he added:

— Oasis Ghat. It has happened.

— Splendid, I am paying for your milk, — Jens Boot replied

Or course, all that could not possibly be known by the special correspondent of "Le Temps." As for Jens Boot, he preferred not to familiarize the public with his business.

Jens Boot felt sad despite of success of his enterprise. He roamed among the people that have lost their memory and yearned forgetfulness himself.

— Lucie... Europe... Love... How can I forget you?

But even fleas have their preferences. Apparently they didn't like Jens's northern body.

Once on April 17 Jens Boot felt an especially acute paroxysm of melancholy and decided to visit Francesco Bari to talk about Europe's past with him. What can be sweeter for an unhappy lover than recalling the golden days of his youth?

Alas, Jens Boot was not about to find consolation for his desperate heart. What he saw at Francesco Bari's apartment had upset him even more. The great philosopher was sitting upon some children's contraption with only his shirt on and sang a silly song:

— Uno, due, tre. Café! Café! Café!

Quatro, cinque, sei. Lei, lei, lei!

— I have come to talk with you about Europe, signor Bari, about transience and essence, — Jens Boot said politely.

But he only heard a toddler's babble in response.

— Want to play hide-and-seek? — offered Francesco Bari and crawled under the bed before even hearing an answer. His silver-grey locks were mopping the floor.

Jens Boot tried to bring the philosopher to his normal state. He reminded him of dear names

— Montjoie ... Renaissance... romantics... Lutetia...

But Francesco Bari just smiled carefree and played with the tail of his shirt.

Suddenly something human twinkled in his eyes, he slapped his forehead and cried out in agony:

— I don't remember! I don't remember anything!

But in a minute an idiotic smile has eclipsed his agony and the philosopher resumed his singing:

— Uno, due, tre. Café, café, café!

Jens Boot went out. He left Rome. Beautiful Campagna was around him. It was roamed by cows They weren't milked for a long time which made them mad. They attacked rare passersby.

Some Romans were roaming Campagna as well. They were searching for their offices and shops among the ancient ruins.

— Where is the ball-bearing warehouse "Electra"? — asked one man.

Those were the ones afflicted with ciquita who have lost their memory. And Jens envied them.

— If only I could get ciquita! — he whispered at his worst moments.

By his destiny, that has always been benevolent to that adventurer, refused him that favor.

Suddenly Jens saw slightly pink warm marble in the grass. It was covered with rusty leaves of many autumns and with grey down of the earth. But how could Jens Boot not recognize his love, the beautiful Phoenician Europe?

People who went to the port of Ostia to leave tender Europe bound for the shores of Asia and Africa used to pray here to Jupiter's lover.

The marble Phoenician smelled the sweet aroma and felt the warmth of sacred burners two thousand years ago. But she had never before knew a kind of fervor that now went through all the bluish veins of her marble body. It was the great eccentric that has failed to catch ciquita who was kissing Europa.

24
Jens Boot Discovers
the teachings of Julio Jurenito

The head was subjected to the cleansing operation right after the arm. Ciquita has easily migrated from Genoa to Barcelona. Iberian Peninsula that was preoccupied with corrida and juntas just six months before forgot about everything. It was desolate, rusty, and wild. Only the gangs of Basques that for some reason got ciquita in a mild form descended the Pyrenees, went south and roamed Andalusia. They fed on figs and shrieked like mules.

Ciquita has not crossed the Pyrenees, and beautiful motherland of m-r Felix Brandeveaux could boast its immortality once again.

Jens Boot was in Amiens. He was looking, contemplating, calculating: the fifth act should not be disappointing to the esteemed audience.

In the evenings after finishing his day's work he was wistful. His character got darker every year. The spectacle of so many calamities has coarsened his once tender heart. Until that memorable evening at the tavern "Pleasant rendezvous" when Choog the floor waxer was looking at the mirror puzzled by his powdered face Jens Boot was capable of mercy and remorse. But seeing that powder of m-r Felix Brandeveaux Jens Boot got petrified forever. Of course, he still could pity signora Lucia, but that pity has not stopped him from inventing a dozen of new ciquitas.

He did not even cast his eyes down and stepped aside. On the contrary, he always hurried to the country that was chosen next ignoring all the perils. Being well informed about the intimacies of the ministries and general staffs he was never late. It wasn't the executioner's lust, nor businessman's jealousy. It was the fate.

Two people lived in Jens Boot: great adventurer, an heir to Napoleon, Jupiter incarnate, Europe's murderer, Director of "D. E. Trust Co." prepared, ordered and supervised precise execution of his orders with a slight smirk. That was one person. The other was a sentimental salesman in love with some French girl, who executed the will of Herr Krieger, who carried signora Lucia's basket, who sighed recalling his favorite pajamas and who wept on the slightest occasion.

One person was not an obstacle for the other. Both put the same signature on the "Trust Co." circulars and love letters alike: Jens Boot.

The only thing that was lacking was an idea. To tell the truth, its absence did not serve as an obstacle for Jens to execute his plans. But people like him have to think about the future. How could Jens Boot answer Americans of XXI century if they asked him: "why have you destroyed Europe?" It wouldn't do giving them incomprehensible confessions about Lucie's fore lock...

Jens Boot lacked the idea. And he stumbled upon it by sheer accident. It happened at boring provincial Amiens.

On a quiet September evening having finished his letters Jens fell into his usual melancholy. Of course, he was recalling his deep disappointment at that Venetian palazzo that once belonged to Marquis Fermuccini. Not catching ciquita then he tried a more conventional way to attain oblivion. M-me Blancafort turned out to be a fat disfigured woman with bad peroxide. Jens went to a first-class bordello that belonged to American firm "Cool & Co." searching for a slim girl with natural hair color. Jens Boot's expedition was a modest success. He got the appropriate consolation from Mlle. Julie — a polite, red-haired person. But Jens devoted and unflippant heart was soon aching again. Mlle. Julie was sound asleep and Jens Boot in his light-blue underpants and a mesh on his head (he always wore it at night to save the hair parting) paced the room and sighed:

— Lucie! That's not what I need... Where are you, my Phoenician?

The Phoenician was next to him and inside him, she was stretching her arms toward the seas — to the southern one full of shells and octopi, to the northern one full of silver herring, she was pushing her feet against that famous pillar where a sparrow had roosted. But Jens Boot did not remember that. He saw the "Tea Star" and sharp teeth biting on an almond cooky. Jens Boot was pacing the room. He could not sleep. Suddenly he noticed a worn dog-eared book on a shelf above the bed. The book's cover had an inscription in etched golden letters:

ATTENTION MESSRS. CLIENTS!

This highly scientific opus advertises our hygienic and aesthetic establishment.

Knowing that bordellos of "Cool & Co." have world-renowned reputation and are highly recommended by many scientists Jens Boot just yawned: must be something medical...

But he opened the book and read it cover to cover standing by a dim night lamp next to Mlle. Julie who slept like a baby.

It was a biography of Great Teacher Julio Jurenito, who had been killed in 1921 at the town of Konotop, and also some of his selected teachings.

Several times Jens Boot stopped reading and swore:
— That sniveller could only philosophize when it was necessary to act!

— What a strange phantasy — to drag seven absolute idiots with you!

— To die for a pair of boots! What a fool! It's like me dying for pajamas...

But those sacrilegious words were prompted by lucid sublime feeling: Jens Boot became a devout disciple of the Great Provocateur.

Moreover, he realized that his entire life — from the swallowed lobster's antenna to the visit to "Cool & Co." bordello is nothing but realization of Julio Jurenito's divine idea.

Jens Boot knew now why he was destroying Europe. Standing at the window that was already turning light blue in his light-blue underpants, shivering, and deeply touched he was repeating unforgettable words of late Mexican:

"No, not hate — the greatest unlove had emptied my heart... And yet it will come — the hour of freedom, exultation, and thoughtlessness..."

— Why haven't you lived till nowadays, Teacher? — Jens whispered. — But rest in peace: there won't be any monument of your killer erected in 1970. In 1970 there only will be sun, St. John's wort and birds' chirping in Europe.

And squinting one eye smartly he went on:

— You loved her too! You left your native Mexico for her... Dying at dirty Konotop for a pair of those boots you saw the proud plod of Phoenician... Rest assured, I shall conquer her!

It was the great minute.

25
What Sometimes Falls from the Skies

France was almost immortal. All rentiers asked to be buried in Pantheon while still alive. But such an exceptional luck always disturbs peace of mind and France was uneasy not knowning what other country can be destroyed. It seemed like all countries of Europe were already destroyed. Just some meager crumbs were left.

In 1935 m-r Felix Brandeveaux decided to pick up the remaining scraps. Switzerland and Belgium were annexed by France within eleven minutes. Holland refused to agree with an edict that was turning it into French department Dune.

After rummaging through the archives Dutch journalists wrote some dubious articles about flooding their country. What did those people hoped for in their efforts to defend their country's independence remained a mystery to us. Maybe the spirit of the great seafarers of yore was still alive in them and they hoped to sail somewhere to another hemisphere taking their country with them. At any rate m-r Felix Brandeveaux was seriously offended learning about Dutch resistance. He didn't want a war. He became a pacifist long time ago. Besides, the declaration of war meant to disturb peace of mind of sympathetic Americans a great deal. M-r Felix Brandeveaux decided to settle the conflict by family means.

— Please, take care of Holland, — he told his war minister general Legate.

— Holland? And what's there? Mountains? Fleet? — asked diligent minister.

— There is rain and cheese.

— As for cheese, I am not a connoisseur. But rain, but rain... I'll take care of the rain...

— Just do it quietly, — m-r Felix Brandeveaux warned him. — We cannot offend Americans.

That conversation took place on August 18, 1935. On August 19 "Le Journal de Debats" wrote:

"Some quite authoritative sources report that French government has peaceful disposition toward Holland and is not about to implement any military measures. If tiny Holland does not understand the economic and moral advantages of its merger with France, we may only pity that country. At any rate, there will be no war."

— There will be no war! — the newspaper peddlers cried in the streets of Paris and Amsterdam.

They we correct. There wasn't any war indeed.

However, Jens Boot hastily sailed to Holland. But this trip was only due to a natural desire to visit his mother Anna Boot, whom he hasn't seen for thirty-four years.

In Holland Jens Boot saw what he was meant to see, that is rain and cheese.

(M-r Felix Brandeveaux new geography quite well).

Jens Boot went directly to the island of Texel without stopping elsewhere. Great catastrophes happened somewhere. Almost all Europe has perished. "D.E Trust company" was still working full time. But here the seabirds still laid their eggs. and the locals ate tasty fried eggs.

Jens entered the small modest house with extremely poignant feeling. Anna Boot was praying. Tall Jens knelt down and kissed his mother's wrinkled hands. When he swallowed lobster's antenna thirty-eight years ago it was very painful and his Mommy tried to console him. And now after M-me Lucie Blancafort cheated him and after he saw Europe in death throes, he needed his mother's consolation more than ever.

Smelling Anna's dress with its aroma of soap and fish Jens recalled his childhood.

Director of "D. E. Trust co." felt himself a little boy again.

Anna Boot dropped her prayer book. That man who just came to her house reminded her of that fleeting but grave sin committed long time ago when she was young.

— Good Lord, help me and have mercy on me, — she whispered.

— Mommy, I am your son Jens!

— That's a lie! You are the seducer, — Anna Boot replied with great suspicion.

Jens had to show her a birthmark on his belly and also a passport. The old woman began to kiss Jens's gloomy bony face then and burst in tears.

It was still raining. Anna Boot asked him anxiously looking at his elegant suit:

— What have you been doing, Jens?

"D. E. Trust Co." executive director did not want to upset his old mother. He answered casually:

— I used to work as a masseur and a hunter. Now I manage a small funeral parlor.

Saying that Jens Boot tried to look aside. Mother's heart is very insightful. Anna Boot told her son:

— You have lied to me, Jens. Perhaps you grew up to be a thief or, Lord helps us, a killer?

Anna Boot was weeping. It was still raining. Jens wanted to confess all his sins to his mother, to lay in his child's bed, eat a big seabird's egg and fall asleep forever. But he was able to overcome that natural yearning.

In the evening Anna Boot got tired with all the events of the day and dozed off in her armchair. Jens went out. It was raining non-stop. However, in this country it can go on for three months on end and it wasn't the rain that stunned him. He witnessed a very strange picture: all the seashore was covered with dead seabirds. They were falling down from the skies like stones just in front of his eyes. When Jens came back to the house his mother was awake, she heard the squeak of the door. Jens decided to share with her what he just saw outside:

— Mommy, all the seashore is covered with the bodies of dead birds. They fall down from the skies. What could it possibly mean?

Anna Boot burst into tears once again.

— It means that you've brought bad luck to my house. Birds have never died here before. You are not my son but the devil!

With those words of his mother Jens Boot, "D. E. Trust Co." executive director began trembling like a child who just have heard a scary tale. Superstitious fear enveloped him. Could it really be that he is a cursed man who has brought the woe to his old mother?

Jens was trembling. His mother was weeping. It was still raining.

— Give me a glass of water, — asked Anna Boot through tears. — Devil, gimme water! Don't try to deceive me! Gimme water, not you devilish poison.

Jens went outside, turned the well's wheel, and brought his mother a glass of fresh cold water.

— Drink, Mommy, — he said with utmost tenderness. His fingers were still trembling.

Anna Boot drank half a glass. She was sitting silent in her armchair. In half an hour terrible grimace has distorted her face. The glass fell down and shattered. She began vomiting.

— You've deceived me, Jens! You gave poison to your mother!

Those were the last words of Anna Boot. Jens fled. He was all alone on the island covered with dead birds.

— Oh! Oh! Oh!

Some fisherman took him back to the continent. He did not answer any questions. He did not see people. He just kept seeing the scared face of his mother and a glass of clear water.

People and animals were dying all around him, in the cities and villages alike. Holland that didn't want to merge with great France was dying in convulsions with froth on her lips.

In Utrecht young Wilhelmina Maastroot was reading a tale to her little daughter beautiful Delie:

— ... And a little blue star has fallen down from the skies...

— Mommy, do the stars indeed fall from the skies?

— Yes, they do, Delie. There is God in the skies. Anything can fall from there...

And finishing the tale she gave Delie Danish King's drops. Delie had a little cough. In a space of five minutes there was a small curled dead body found in the crib.

The rain was still falling. Jens Boot ran across wet fields, fell several times, then ran on, ran and cried:

— Oh! Oh! Oh!

This time he obviously wished something impossible: he tried to run away from himself.

In a matter of two weeks there were no people left in Holland. It was still raining. Warehouses were full of red mountains of uneaten cheese.

One little note has survived with some other papers of m-r Felix Brandeveaux:

"Three hundred devices... In the clouds at their formation... Rain... Six days."

But it is at least indecent to read other people's letters. There was no war. American pacifists sent m-r Felix Brandeveaux congratulatory letter along with a dove made of solid gold...

26
"A Hundred 'Aphros' at once..."

On May 22, 1937 the walls and fences of Perpignan were decorated with beautiful tricolor placards:

DEAR CITIZENS!

Our Fatherland is in danger!

Beginning with April 1936 the office of civil acts has not registered a single birth in Perpignan.

What will happened with our beautiful Perpignan in twenty years? Who is going to vote in Parliamentary elections? Who will read our respected newspaper "L'hote de Perpignan"? Who will drink our great aperitifs that are not falsified?

Citizens, wake up!

The city Council has decreed that any citizen who is capable of becoming a father will be awarded one hundred gold francs and a diploma of honor. The ceremony will take place at the main assembly room of the city hall. The final decision will be made by the jury presided by Dr. Le Quichotte, the city physician. Candidates must register at the secretary's office.

Hurry up, dear citizens!

Hurry up before it's too late!

We trust in your masculinity!

Mayor of Perpignan
Alphonse Mairedeault

Compatriots of Mairedeault crowded near those placards all day long.

— In exactly two hundred and seventy days there will be no less than ten thousand babies born in Perpignan, — young and beautiful notary public named Ballier was boasting. — I don't go to register just because I don't like to wait in line, — there must be a stampede there today.

But m-r Ballier was wrong. Mayor's secretary was looking at the window all day long, all hope being lost. There was just dogs' marriage in the square. Dogs were barking merrily. The secretary yawned. No candidate has shown up.

We would like to warn the reader not to make a wrong conclusion that Perpignan was an exceptionally sinful city that was punished for its transgressions. No, the same picture could be observed all over France:

1) Midwives went totally unemployed;

2) The streets everywhere were quiet since the citizens of tender age were entirely missing;

3) All elementary schools were converted into dancing classes for adults;

4) Toys manufacturers were committing suicide on a regular basis, etc.

An historian is no bashful girl. It is his duty to open the veil that separates us from the life of societies of yore mercilessly, and he is not the one to be blamed for the discrepancies between that life and the fundamental principles of goodness and decency. Our duty is to find the causes that has led France to such an abnormal situation.

The leading cause was certainly war. France was fighting wars for twenty-five years almost without interruption. It kept millions of its citizens mobilized. Young boys drafted hastily at the age of fifteen were corrupted immediately. Quartermaster service was responsible for supply and maintenance of 4800 stationary and 17,600 mobile bordellos for soldiers. It is quite easy to imagine how all that affected the sanitary condition of population at large. By 1935 statistics had already shown the drop in the birth rate of 48%.

Then the rescue came about in the form of medication. The owner of large chemical factory "D.E." began production of golden pills named "Aphroditine." This medicine contained some esters along with testicular extracts. It was designed to serve three purposes: it helped to overcome bashfulness, prevented pregnancies and therefore the budgetary burdens and caused euphoria, just like any narcotic. "D.E." factory was swamped with orders. Its owners soon became the richest people in France. As for the public at large, it has fallen in love with "Aphroditine" and for the sake of convenience called it just "Aphro."

The pills were gilded with harmless bronze powder and sold in an attractive package. Brides presented their bridegrooms with the neat boxes of pills. Caring mothers-in-law always bought a box of "Aphro" while making their usual shopping tour to the market. The waiters at the bars would order a bartender when they served a couple: "Two picon curacaos — two! One 'Aphro' — one!"

Soldiers, those natural carriers of the city culture, had familiarized the countryside dwellers with the charms of "Aphro." At every tiny village shop that served the needs of fishermen in Brittany or shepherds in Savoy one could find those universally yearned pills.

The government of m-r Felix Brandeveaux was much too busy wiping out other countries as well as exterminating remaining communists, and therefore did not interfere with citizens' private life. As readers could see it was a liberal government indeed.

"Aphro" became the hero. Voluminous scientific treatises were written about it. Frivolous songs were composed. In 1936 alone fourteen million neat boxes containing those pills were sold. At the annual meeting of the "D.E." factory stockholders only one word was heard: "Triumph!"

The stockholders cordially thanked the new director of the factory m-r Jens Boot, who has bought a patent for that magnificent "Aphro." M-r director was greatly touched.

By that time the new yet unknown properties of that magic drug became quite obvious. After three to four boxes "Aphro" turned a young healthy robust man into a perfect eunuch. At first the "Aphro" addicts felt some fatigue and intense head-ache. They had to increase the dose. Some took up to eight or even ten pills at a time. Finally, the drug stopped working completely and anyone who had hoped for its beneficial effect had to retreat in shame.

After all the ministers, the ministers' sons, nephews and even some grandsons experienced the destructive effects of "Aphro" on themselves the government showed some interest in the dangerous manufacturer. Prosecutor general came to Lille where "D.E." factory was located. He found out that the factory director m-r Jens Boot left the day before and that his whereabouts were unknown.

Manufacturing of "Aphro" was prohibited under the threat of death penalty. Unfortunately, it was too late. Hardly twen-ty thousand men that had not experienced the hopes and dis-appointments of "Aphro" could be found in all of France. The vast majority of French men had to accept their sad fate.

The same could not be said about French women. Mental disorders among them became very common. Maternity hos-pitals were converted into psychiatric wards.

The bravest women ran away from their homes and reached the country's borders where the wilderness began. They wait-ed until dark. The border patrols were ordered to shoot any-one who dared to cross the border. The brave runaways crawled over deep border trenches at night. Many have perished. The ones that reached their goal stripped themselves naked and waited for savages to come. France was brimming with the leg-ends of brave barbarians that seemed to abduct women, or so they said. As a matter of fact, some people who roamed the wilderness — Basques, Ligurians or Swabians — sometimes re-warded French women for their true heroism. But the majority of them have perished of cold or were devoured by wild animals that quite audaciously moved to the very borders of France.

Such was the state of affairs at the beginning of 1937. "Aphro" has completely met the expectations of the "D.E." fac-tory's diligent director.

The Chamber of Deputies introduced an emergency bill that proposed importation of two hundred thousand Negroes from the colonies to France. The bill supposed that after the use of obedient savages' breeding potential they would be concentrated at one of the peripheries of republic and then exterminated so that they could not cause the lawful white husbands the paroxysms of excessive jealousy. The bill was met with fierce resistance of French Academy. "The Immortals" stated that the new generation would not be purely white and saw the betrayal of Latin race's venerable traditions in it. Progressive circles, on the contrary, were welcoming the change of color. The song dedicated to the Republic was sung at cabarets:

> Marianne! Marianne!
> You'll be café au lait...

The bill was declined by 316 votes against 174 (316 "traditional" deputies were married, 174 were free-thinking bachelors).

The newly created ministry of popular proliferation decided then to propose the appropriate competitions to the mayors and prefects of certain towns and cities.

The mayor of Perpignan m-r Mairdeault has composed the inspiring placard that was shown in the opening lines of this chapter after reading the minister's circular.

It was the first competition, and all France held her breath following its results. Special correspondents of all major Parisian newspapers came to Perpignan.

Correspondent of "Le Petit Journal" m-r Gropette was ahead of his colleagues and composed his first cable right on his arrival at the train station:

"The stream of candidates is so great that the city council had to employ military guards and firefighters to maintain order. The number of candidates has surpassed twenty thousand. Gorgeous weather is of great help for coming events."

M-r Gropette got a shave after that, ate his breakfast and went to the city hall. The secretary was sitting by the window yawning. The big list where the candidates were supposed to sign in was pristinely clean.

M-r Gropette composed the second cable:

"The situation got somewhat complicated due to foreign subterfuge. The spies from Chita had been arrested. The weather is still favorable. France will be victorious!"

M-r Mairdeault ordered all the officials of the city hall to leave everything and devote themselves to the search for a single man who never took "Aphro." The officials ran, sweated and sighed. Gropette cabled:

"We need the nerves of steel in order to win."

The proper man was nowhere to be found. At last, on May 29 an old city hall watchman Leon brought a nice-looking bashful youth, who led modest life with his elderly grandmother, cultivated beans and potatoes, believed in God and had never seen the gilded pills. It was truly unexpected joy. M-r Mairdeault hugged the youth pressing him against his tricolor-wrapped belly and doused him with a shower of patriotic tears:

— You are Charlemagne, you are Joan d'Arc, you are Danton, you are m-r Felix Brandeveaux, — he whispered in utter delight to bashful youth whose name was Paul Petit.

Further description of the events we'll grant to the poetic pen of m-r Gropette:

Fourth cable:

"Paul Petit is beautiful and bold. His bride, the daughter of m-r Mairdeault is the most beautiful and honest girl in the city. Other cities ought to follow the example of Perpignan. We'll conquer the whole world. There is a huge flow of American tourists. All the hotels are booked to the capacity."

Fifth cable:

"City hall is decorated with flags and illuminated with electric monograms. The square is full of joyful people. The popular entertainments were organized: carousels and target shooting. Military orchestra is playing. The bride is at the hall already. Paul Petit is finishing his supper under physicians' supervision."

Sixth cable:

"Paul Petit ate two soft boiled eggs, spinach and de volaille cutlet, drank a glass of mineral water. The orchestra played flourish of trumpets."

Seventh cable:

"Paul Petit is led to the hall. He tries to resist due to quite understandable bashfulness."

Eighth cable:

"Paul Petit sat on a step and asked permission to smoke a cigarette. The orchestra is playing "Toreador.""

Ninth cable:

"Paul Petit is still sitting. The weather is still favorable. Perpignan has excellent carousels. A spy from Chita has been apprehended."

Tenth cable:

"Elation! Hellas! Gallic rooster! Paul Petit has entered the hall. The doors have been sealed. The crowd keeps reverent silence. Evoe!"

The editors' board was waiting for the most important eleventh cable in vain. There was none. The pen has betrayed m-r Gropette. He could not give description of the consummation of that solemn night.

Exactly at 12:00 midnight when the orchestra was playing "La Marseillaise"

Paul Petit's miserable mug showed up in the window. The youth tried in vain to open the sealed and firmly locked doors and therefore had to use the window. He was weeping desperately and cried through tears:

"A hundred "Aphros," at once!"

But no "Aphro" could help the last hero of France.

27

"It is necessary to shave the dog"

Of all operations conducted by "D. E. Trust Co." extermination of the peoples that once inhabited Scandinavian peninsula remains the most mysterious one. No historian was able to elucidate that curious albeit not the most important question so far. This can be explained not by any particular complexity of Scandinavian operation but just by sad eventuality. When the secret archive of "D. E. Trust Co." was discovered in 2004, the folder # 18621 that contained all the documents concerned with events of 1938 was missing. Archive was kept at Mr. Twyweight's safe. Therefore, we cannot suspect either thieves or mice. No, the only one guilty for that loss was late Mr. Twyweight himself who used to like going through those touching and instructive documents. So it happened that he went on his usual morning trip to the kitchen garden establishment taking the folder #18621 with him and came back home without the papers. Such incidents happen due to absentmindedness every now and then even with the best people. But alas, because of that naïve gesture of Mr. Twyweight we cannot show the necessary details of Scandinavian demise.

We were able to get hold of only six documents that we cite in their entirety.

I. Jens Boot's notebook in an oilcloth cover. Page # 41 has a note written with ink pencil:

"November 26, 1936. Watched "Brand." Provincial fool. Cream and sour cream + implacable attitude toward his lawful spouse. As a matter of fact, remembered: it is necessary to shave the dog. NB!"

II. Cables to various American newspapers sent in March 1938 from Stockholm, Copenhagen and Christiania:

"Some cases of sleeping sickness are detected. Measures were undertaken. Quarantine at the Danish borders implemented."
"Vaccinations were implemented at schools."
"According to specialists' opinion the mild forms of sleeping sickness were observed in the past. In 1922 mild outbreaks happened in Moscow and New York City".
"Mortality is growing."
"American government issued a prohibition for all vessels to enter Scandinavian ports."
"Epidemic is unraveling to the ominous levels."
"Communication by mail has been interrupted."

III. Letters of Danish artist Johann Alsay to M-me Gabrielle Bonot in Paris.
Letter #1.

"Gabrielle, I am writing to you from Tivoli. We used to sit on that bench together. Do you remember it, behind a small kiosk? You've been showing me you red gloves with tufts that looked like puma's ears. I wanted to paint you then with your green jumper on. Children were crying. Now it is very quiet here. Young man with a tennis racquet sits on the bench next to mine. He opens his mouth all the time. But don't imagine that he is singing or yelling. No, he is just yawning like everyone in this green, glassy and watery Copenhagen. It means that in a week the orderlies in face masks will haul his body to a crematorium. The orderlies, however, will also want to sleep. Gabrielle, do you know what sleep is? Light, jingling, whitish like this city. When eyes see the abyss and a cigarette falls out of your fingers. Oh, sleep, sleep!.. My poor girl, if you could only see how I want to sleep!..

But no, don't be afraid. I am completely healthy. I can run and cry. I can love. More than ever. I walk along the empty tinny canals of the port. North Sea smells of dampness and silence. I am searching for your lips, your tarry dry bitter southern lips, Gabrielle! I have decided to leave everything. I shall come to you. It is not easy, or so they say. But that's nonsense. I have to be with you. Do you remember that night in Esbjerg when the siren was howling and the stars were falling from the skies like a golden hail. I realized even then — that was not just love — something else. If not us, then who? A man with a racquet will fall asleep now. They all will. And we must endure... No, I don't know how to write about that. I shall tell you when I see you, I shall breathe it in the pink shell of your ear. Gabrielle, we shall call him Sandro!..

I shall not go to bed tonight. I shall stay on guard. Gabrielle, kiss me!"

Letter #2

"Gabrielle, I am coming to you. I have been fighting that deceptive breath of water all day long. It is easy to understand — even the sea is yawning. June. White nights. I have to pinch myself not to fall asleep. I have found a boat. I shall depart in the evening. I can hear Paris. Italian boulevards. Humming of steel beetles. Clanking of glasses at the cafes. Laughter. Cafes at your place are open till the morning, aren't they? If only I can stay awake! Your lips, Gabrielle! Just don't let me fall asleep! In three short hours I shall embark. The boatsman is asleep. Orderlies wearing face masks in a truck. Pastor is riding with them. He is yawning too. You must know that feeing — when feet are getting pleasantly cool and your head feels as if somebody is pouring thick viscous honey all over it. No, that is — death!.. I plead with you — wake me up!.."

Letter #3

"It's time to go. I can't. Mommy used to make honey gingerbread — elephant with a trunk. The trunk was the tastiest part. Do you remember how I kissed you shoulder and you laughed: "I want to sleep." My dear, I want it too! Everyone is asleep. Too late. Good night. There is a man in a face mask standing over me. It seems like..."

IV. Chicago magazine "Worldwide," issue # 316 gives a description of the sleeping sickness:

"Symptoms: pallor, swollen face. Eyes go dim. Movements are sluggish. Sudden somnolence. Weak pulse.
Natural course: yawning. Sleep for up to twenty hours a day. In the first few days of illness patients still wake up to eat. Then the sleep goes on without waking.
The microbes of sleeping sickness cause fatty degeneration of the muscles within 14–18 days".

V. Report of the last session of Norway's Storting on October 29, 1938.

Chairman: I declare the session open.
Voices: There is no quorum.
Chairman: Eighty-nine deputies have passed away. Let us honor them by standing up.
Voices from the left: the right keeps sitting
Deputy Hopson (conserve.): The only one who is sitting is deputy Trollke. He is asleep.
Intermission. Orderlies carry deputy Trollke away.
Chairman: Deputy Argen is recognized for 5 minutes.
Deputy Argen (extreme left). The country is dying. Fatty degeneration is caused by the excesses of bourgeoisie.

We cannot wait any longer. Representing my party, trade unions and factory committees I declare the government null and void. Storting is dissolved. The authority is passed to...

Confusion in the audience. Deputy Argen suddenly goes silent.

Chairman: Esteemed deputy Argen, you are still recognized for three minutes.

Deputy Argen is silent.

Deputy Tulby (soc.-dem.) We plead with you colleague Argen to tell us who is now holding the authority. It is extremely important.

Chairman: Alas, deputy Argen cannot answer. Deputy Argen is asleep.

Orderlies carry deputy Argen away.

Chairman (yawning): I declare the session closed. I want to sleep.

VI. Cable of Mr. York, special correspondent of "Free Associated Press of America."

"Major sensation! No live person is left in Scandinavia. I have made seven sorties today. I have seen dead Copenhagen. Sun was shining on the cathedral's spire. Cows are roaming all over Denmark. They are awake. Stockholm is as quiet as paradise. Faces of some sleepers smile blissfully. The demise of this nation is a triumph of pure spiritualism. I've witnessed the last minutes of the last man. What a beauty! It was a fisherman at Trolberg fjord. He sailed to his morning harvest. The water was turquoise, the sun was pure gold. The fisherman pulled his net. Silver fish was fluttering. He sighed quietly, closed his eyes with his arm and fell asleep. Fell asleep instantly, just like a baby. The net went back in the water. The fish had escaped merrily. The fisherman was sleeping under the golden sun, over the turquoise waters. Evangelical dreams! Holy Fisherman! No doubt that we'll soon begin colonization of these lands. The grand scale disinfection is necessary first. There are lots of raw materials here: iron, copper, timber. I saw death. Life will come back. Good morning, dear readers!"

28

"SORE"

On June 30, 1928, when Herr Krieger was dying in the ruins of Berlin, Victor Brandeveaux was standing in one of the tanks. Prime minister's nephew was looking down the black tunnel of millennia with glassy empty stare. What he saw was terrible indeed. Sun was cooling down quickly, it was hanging in the icy sky like a huge egg yolk. The earth was covered with cacti and gigantic moss and pressed upon by mammoths, kangaroo-rats, tortoises and giant spiders. Then the sun went out altogether. Blind dwarves with faces covered in bristly red hair crawled over the lichens. At times they lunged at each other crying "choo-choo" and sucked warm thick blood. Second lieutenant of French army Victor Brandeveaux looked at those monsters for a long time. He was trying to understand who they were: our great grandfathers or the great grandsons?

When at dawn the tanks moved back having finished the destruction of Berlin, Victor Brandeveaux was lying down with his eyes shut and raved. He was placed at the best hospital in Liege. A month later m-r Felix Brandeveaux came to Liege to decorate his heroic nephew with a military medal of honor. The hospital was decorated splendidly and all the hotels of Liege were full of foreign correspondents. But the ceremony was overshadowed by the most mysterious events. When the prime minister finished his passionate speech and came to the bed to kiss the sick soldier he found there just an incongruous effigy.

Victor Brandeveaux has disappeared in the most mysterious way to sheer joy of detectives and journalists worldwide who got occupied with that matter for quite some time. We have already mentioned that the newspaper "Le people" had asserted that Dutch adventurer Jean Botha was no one else than Victor Brandeveaux, who had disappeared under mysterious circumstances. Our readers that are well familiar with Jens Boot's biography don't need any proofs of the simple fact that mixing of these two persons is quite unbecoming.

We could not find out with certainty what Victor Brandeveaux was doing for all those ten years. We only knew that in 1932 he was at St. Ignatius monastery near Salamanca where he had amazed other monks with the fervor of his prayers and severity of his pledges. At the confession brother Hippolyte (that was Victor Brandeveaux's assumed name at the time of his becoming a monk) had admitted that he had killed billions of people including some Pharaoh Pherunkhanun, the owner of cabaret "Al Casar" and his great grandson — the dwarf covered in bristly red fur.

Three years later we find Victor Brandeveaux in a very different environment, namely — among the students of higher military academy in Tomsk. He lives there under his proper name as a political emigrant, earns his living by teaching French and studies chemistry and electric engineering.

These are all the data that we have about the life of Victor Brandeveaux. We do not intend to bring our scientific study to the level of psychological novel therefore, we shall not attempt to elucidate emotional tribulations of that passionate young man that have led him on his very convoluted way from the tank to the monastery of St. Ignatius and from a confession booth to the lab at the military academy in the most politically suspect state. We also don't know how Victor Brandeveaux has managed to return to his native country. But on April 12, 1939 at the meeting of unemployed held at the grand hall of Labor exchange in Paris a gaunt dark man wearing a cap was giving a speech. He yelled shaking his fists:

— Comrades! French bourgeoisie having destroyed Europe now began its attack on ourselves. Our grandfathers had responded to the treachery of bourgeois with Paris Commune.

Comrades, Chita will help us! America is on the brink of social revolution. Japan is in vague discontent as well! There are reliable data that some live oases remain in European wilderness. These unfortunates who have survived all the horrors of wars and epidemics will help us to overthrow the yoke of capitalism.

Be brave! Take to the streets! We need a singular plan of action. Long live "Syndicate Ouvrier pour Retablissement de Europe"!

Four thousand unemployed who attended the meeting met the passionate speaker with wild applause. Perhaps, the monks of St. Ignatius monastery who had perished of ciquita would disapprove the immoral character of his speech but they, no doubt, would have appreciated the exceptional pathos that was inherently present in brother Hippolyte. As for the unemployed, they really didn't care for Victor Brandeveaux's oratorical mastery. No, they simply were very hungry. They were doomed. A strange man wearing a cap has suggested some kind of escape. He even promised the help of Russians, Americans, Japanese and European savages — help of everybody. Only one thing remained to be done, that is — the former manufacturer of tin boxes m-r Felix Brandeveaux has to be done for.

When the unemployed have resolved to do exactly that and took to the streets singing "International" a small police detachment dispersed them in a matter of few minutes with a help of poison gas. Two hundred and forty people were poisoned to death. The ranks of the parasites living on poor m-r Felix Brandeveaux's dole have shrunk by two hundred and forty souls. But it was little consolation. If two hundred and forty perished there still remained three million one hundred and ten thousand living on a government's dole.

No wonder then that m-r Felix Brandeveaux felt the yoke of power tragically getting heavier by the day. The situation of Great France who had defeated all her enemies was far from being enviable.

We have already mentioned the hardships of the government caused by almost complete absence of births in the country. In 1939 m-r Felix Brandeveaux finally ignored all the resolutions of the Chamber of Deputies and imported about a hundred thousand Senegalese men to France for procreation. But the Negroes grew insolent after experiencing some minutes of domination over white women and were probably instigated by the agents of Chita government to mutiny. They disturbed m-r Felix Brandeveaux's tranquility day in and day out.

The unemployed behaved even worse than Negroes. French industry has perished entirely after losing all export markets and foreign sources of raw materials. Saint Etienne, Lille, Nancy and other industrial centers looked like antics museums. They even became attractions for American tourists. Many workers were wearing military long coats.

Fearing invasion of barbarians and internal turmoil France maintained gigantic army. Its numbers reached two million and eight hundred thousand by 1935. But m-r Felix Brandeveaux was smart enough not to recruit all the unemployed. He kept feeding more than three million idlers: it was not as dangerous as rifles in workers' hands. Sometimes in the hours of insomnia worrying about the fate of his dearly loved motherland that genius of prime minister pulled out "The History of Quelling the Mutiny of 1871" off the shelf and mumbled smugly:

— At any rate — two thirds are more than one third. The peasants will bail us out!

After such a night finance minister in his turn was afflicted with insomnia because he had to add up countless zeroes that made up state budget. Golden reserve has moved to America long time ago. Nobody paid any taxes. The printing presses were issuing billions of francs every day to pay the army and the unemployed. Soldiers were given meat and wine, whereas the unemployed were fed just lentil soup but even a kilo of lentils cost twenty thousand francs, and finance minister had to rub his temples with anti-migraine pencil while working on a budget. Social conflicts have reached exclusive almost picturesque expressivity. Speculative bourgeois tried to spend his trillions as soon as possible having no heirs. All remaining cocottes of Europe came to Paris. They entertained weary Parisians with dances and acrobatics and equilibristic tricks.

Restaurants were full all day long, they didn't even close at night. The last generation of French bourgeoisie was in a hurry to discover all the secrets of all wineries.

Military brass was feasting together with profiteers, they have looted a lot of wealth in the merry military expeditions.

When Mr. Twyweight saw a picture of Parisian restaurant "Mon petit trou" published in Chicago journal "Worldwide" he mumbled amazedly:

— But we are paupers. All America is just a shabby shack compared to that!

France's ruling classes appreciated the situation quite rightly. They didn't want to lose precious time. Need and privation of the unheard proportions were all around them. Millions of unemployed were starving, loitering at the quais and Bois Boulogne parc and shaking their miserable powerless fists. Those creatures hardly resembled civilized people. They wore tatters, covered their unwashed bodies with rags, burlap and old flags. Their heads and faces were covered with uncut and unshaven hair. They long have stopped talking and thinking, just cursed every now and then. They were evicted, moved from one city to another but even that great man who was as brave as ancient heroes m-r Felix Brandeveaux was hesitant to exterminate them entirely. Unemployed were still getting lentil soup. And every kilo of lentils cost twenty thousand francs.

Peasants knew that and they hated the idlers who got lentils for free. Peasants ate meat, bacon and cottage cheese. But peasants had to pay in real louis d'or for American made fabrics. That was quite insulting to them. Peasants loathed the cities.

So, life in France was far from normal. Besides the harsh economic situation France experienced mass neurosis. Nobody knew for sure what was going on outside French borders. Rumors were that the savages of the wilderness got organized and were about to invade eastern and southern departments. The scientists, on the contrary, insisted based on pilots' testimony that the last people in the wilderness have died out completely, that France is surrounded by the plagued lands that are roamed by feral animals. One way or the other every

Frenchman felt horror when he thought of vast expanses that surrounded his country. Life on the small island surrounded by the ocean of death was hard indeed.

A customer at a high-class café would suddenly drop his wine glass and cried in horror: he saw huge void in front of him. It was agoraphobia. Unemployed growled like animals every now and then and pointed to the south or east with their twisted arms covered in red hair winking at each other.

The dread of wilderness grew by the day. M-r Felix Brandeveaux ordered all cities to be illuminated to extinguish night and darkness altogether. Wildly bright artificial moons were glowing. Blindingly bright chandeliers were lit all night long at the prime minister's office. But despite of all that unfathomable and invincible darkness still ruled beyond French borders.

Negroes have finally mutinied in Nice. They slaughtered two thousand eight hundred and sixteen lawful husbands and with widows' consent settled in their villas declaring themselves full-fledged citizens. In Lille the outbreak of typhus aggravated my malnutrition occurred. Third army quartered near the borders of former Spain wanted another looting spree and demanded declaration of war against Morocco that declared independence in 1931. Paris also experienced an obvious mutiny of the unemployed. The meeting where Victor Brandeveaux made his speech was just a beginning of it. Wealthy Parisians were at a loss — they used to treat the unemployed like dirty but harmless animals.

Jens Boot, on the contrary, was quite satisfied with those events. By that time "D. E. Trust Co." director lived very decently residing at the luxurious mansion at Boulevard Saint Germain under the name of Jean de Bouvier, a high-ranking official of the defense ministry. M-r Felix Brandeveaux had not made any important decision without consulting m-r Jean de Bouvier first.

On April 12, 1939 after reading about the first meeting of the unemployed that led to an unsuccessful demonstration Jens Boot stretched himself with pleasure and yawned. This gesture is well familiar to anybody who feels the nearing end of long and hard work. "D. E. Trust Co." director had every right to yawn. He was about to yawn again when the butler came in and said that some visitor needs to see m-r Jean de Bouvier urgently. The visitor's card said:

Pierre Camin, Chaiman
Syndicate of French unemployed

Tall man with dark hair came in. He had not taken his cap off and said:

— Hello, Jens Boot!

Not a single move showed any surprise in m-r Jean de Bouvier whose identity was disclosed so suddenly by a strange visitor. Jens Boot looked carefully at the Pierre Camin's face. He had good memory for faces. He answered his visitor in plain friendly manner:

— Oh, that's you... I think we have met in Tomsk, it seems to me. M-r Victor Brandeveaux? My pleasure. Such a genius of an uncle must have a nephew no less genial.

— Stop playing the ape, — replied Victor Brandeveaux visibly irritated. — I came to you to talk business. I know who you are and what you are doing. You are truly great man. But I want you to do something really deserving of your talents. Let us rebuild Europe.

— And what for, may I ask?

— What for?

Victor Brandeveaux was so surprised by that naïve question, that he fell into a deep thought before answering it.

— Well, to make room for people to live, at the very least. It used to be a pretty decent part of the world. Oh yes, I know your answer to that! Of course, there were lots of ugly things in Europe. But now we'll do everything differently. We'll create a great workers' state. We'll rebuild the cities. We'll extend out hand to fraternal Siberia. Paris is the old fort of revolution. We may unite people of the wilderness around ourselves by overthrowing the power of bourgeoisie.

— I am sorry, — "D. E. Trust Co." director interrupted the young enthusiast politely, — according to the latest data the number of people still alive in the wilderness has been estimated around a few hundred if not a few dozen.

— The new ones will be born! Honest, healthy, hard-working generation!

— My dear young friend, haven't they heard of my patented drug "Aphro" over there in Tomsk?

— It doesn't matter, we'll bring people from all over the world. The main thing is to establish an ideal new order, a realm of justice. Everything else will follow.

Jens Boot offered a cigarette to his guest.

— Please… I am really glad that you have come to me. It is great pleasure to speak to the last dreamer of Europe. However, France has to perish — it is just a leftover trash of yesterday's party. Ventilation is above all! As for re-colonization, America will probably take care of that.

— But how is your America better than Europe?

— I don't know that. Moreover, I don't care. What is "better" or "worse" — damn it? You must've been thoroughly brainwashed at Salamanca and Tomsk. Double nurturing. As for myself, father Francis's pinches made me move hastily to brothers Medrano circus, and in Russia I liked to fight the whites but used to fall asleep at the lectures on historical materialism. "Jedem das Seine" — late Germans used to say. Perhaps, Europe is better than America, you know better than I. I only know one thing: dead Napoleon is usually taken under so he won't stink, and a live kitten is fed warm milk. Bury Europe with any ceremony you like, but do it quickly just out of respect to my sensitive nose.

— Jens Boot, you are the greatest cynic but I don't believe you. Why have you destroyed Europe but left alone other four equally disgusting parts of the world?

— Man's powers are limited, you know. You may strike me four times but I still expect your cordial gratitude for what I have done to Europe.

— Why have you chosen Europe? I have read political speeches of Mr. Jabbs, the diary of Mr. Hardyle and eugenic treatises of Mr. Twyweight — don't they offend your olfactory faculties?

Hearing that decisive question Jens Boot blushed like a girl, cast his eyes down and mumbled quietly:

— Because I love Europe, the Phoenician, true Mlle. Lucie Flamengo.

With this the conversation went into a long pause. Victor Brandeveaux was leafing through an album with the views of Venice, being a really tactful man.

Jens Boot sank into various reminiscences.

Feasters in a brightly lit street sang popular song:

"You are the last chick in Europe, Zip-zip!"

Three hundred kilometers away from Jean de Bouvier study wind roared over terrible wilderness shrouded in darkness.

Finally, Victor Brandeveaux dared to interrupt silence:

— I apologize for being immodest. I understand your feelings. It's all true. But why destroy it?.. It is better to rebuild. There's reason. There's justice after all.

— I can't think. I am not good with numbers. I consider justice to smell of a small shop. Don't be surprised: "D.E Trust co." director is a wild animal, a bull in shirtsleeves. I value only one thing in the whole world — freedom.

Former brother Hippolyte of the monastery of Saint Ignatius, former alumnus of the Academy of Tomsk comrade Victor Brandeveaux jumped off his seat and yelled indignantly:

— Deception! Thousand years old deception! What is freedom? It's fiction!

But Jens Boot interrupted him sternly:

— Young man, freedom isn't something to argue about. A have already told you my main principle: ventilation above all! A question of freedom is a question of fresh air. I sleep with open window all year long. And now — good bye.

M-r Jean de Bouvier pushed a button and bald ancient patrician-like butler escorted citizen Pierre Camin to the door.

— He is a sadist! A madman! A wild bourgeois bastard! — whispered Victor Brandeveaux at the entrance door. — But we shall fight. The workers of Paris will save Europe.

As for Jens Boot he went to the phone immediately after the annoying guest had left and called m-r Felix Brandeveaux despite of late hour.

Prime minister was really worried by the morning demonstration. M-r Jean de Bouvier called him just on time. Their conversation lasted for twenty minutes.

— No concessions, — m-r Jean de Bouvier was saying. — We have army at our disposal. The morale is excellent. I guarantee the results. The best defense is offense. It is necessary to declare the end of all government dole to the unemployed. Meetings and street riots are to be dispersed with the help of gases. In mere two weeks the number of unemployed which now stands at three million will be cut in half. Be brave! Be real Napoleon!

M-r Jean de Bouvier knew how to touch prime minister's heart: after "Napoleon" the problem was solved. The next morning placards were issued that announced a new important government decree. Police had quickly quenched the riots at Montrouge quarters. The day was calm.

In the evening an unknown gaunt and dark-haired soldier came to Vincent barracks where three regiments largely recruited from the ranks of the unemployed had been quartered.

— Now or never, — shouted Victor Brandeveaux at the barrack's courtyard.

An hour later an artillery duel was raging on in Paris. Jens Boot was wiping the lenses of his binoculars with suede.

The soldiers of Paris garrison took the side of the unemployed. The government has fled to Orleans in the middle of the night. Revolutionary Council declared himself the center of "Syndicate Ouvrier pour Retablissement de Europe." The radio message was sent to: "Everyone, everyone."

"Unite, hurry to the aid of worker's Paris! Long live the Pan-European Commune!"

The sign at the façade of former Chamber of Deputies now read:

SORE
"Syndicate Ouvrier pour Retablissement de Europe"

29
Black Tunnel

M-r Felix Brandeveaux safely came to Orleans, drank a glass of picon to brace himself up and commenced to organize the army to quell the mutiny. All troops that were idling at the borders of the wilderness were urgently ordered to march to the interior of the country. The government invited all reasonable and hardworking peasants of France to quell the city-dwelling idlers. By the end of April all France was engaged in civil war. Those were not the make-shift battles of yore but highly elaborate operations of two gigantic armies armed with the latest inventions of all seven departments of defense ministry.

The 2nd and 5th armies that were made up chiefly of worker conscripts took the side of "SORE" in their entirety. They managed to occupy northern France from Paris to former Dutch border. The center and south of the country were, on the contrary, controlled by the forces loyal to the government of m–r Felix Brandeveaux. However, on April 28 the Lyon's garrison mutinied and joined "SORE". The tank brigades that rushed to rescue the government had Lyon razed to the ground. On May 1 riots in Marseille were quenched with poison gases along with all its inhabitants. Eight thousand and six hundred airplanes of which two thousand and one hundred were captured by "SORE" bombed different cities and towns. In May the war became stationary. Ile–de–France, Champagne, Burgundy were scarred with trenches and turned into desert. On May 24 "SORE" troops made a breakthrough and reached Brittany.

The war was of exceptionally brutal character. Peasants killed the city dwellers without mercy. Storming into the cities they methodically gassed one neighborhood after another. Workers loathed greedy stupid country folk. When they seized a farm they burned all the houses and barns, cut the orchards and killed everything that moved, even cats and starlings. The finale was coming fast.

The last American vessel left the shores of Europe on July 14. Jens Boot packed his small suitcase with all his modest belongings: a spare set of underwear, a ticket to "Tea Star," a photograph of unforgettable pajamas and a map of Europe. The great "Whale" airplane was ready to take him.

By early July the army of "SORE" was completely destroyed except for Paris garrison. But even the victorious armies of m–r Felix Brandeveaux had only about a hundred thousand men left, most of them being either very lucky or staff generals. As for so called "civilian population" it has ceased to exist. One could seldom see some crawling or leaping shadows among the ruins. Those were the ones who survived but went mad.

There were no borders anymore. Great European wilderness had devoured France. Wild animals, wind and darkness reigned where the artificial electric moons shone and where choy music was playing so recently.

But Paris still stood in the midst of the wilderness. It was still a living city, real city, European capital. The army of m–r Felix Brandeveaux stood within a hundred kilometers of it. Of course, new Napoleon could have leveled it in two to three hours, but he didn't want to. A man needs shelter to live in. Shelters are located in the houses, and the only livable houses still stood in Paris. That is why m–r Felix Brandeveaux decided to kill a lion without spoiling its magnificent hide.

On April 2, 1939 at 10:00 AM the radio station of Eiffel tower received a following message:

To comrade Victor Brandeveaux,
Chairman of "SORE" council

With sincere remorse and condemnation of our counterrevolutionary fallacies we plead with magnanimous proletariat of Paris to forgive us and accept us in its midst. We hope to redeem ourselves with hard labor in great cause of reconstruction of Europe.

Army Council.

Paris was jubilant. All the streets were decorated with red flags. Parisians met their former enemies with tears and tenderness.

M-r Felix Brandeveaux was a cautious man, so he preferred to enter Paris not astride a white horse but on foot, wearing plain soldier's long coat and even having his gorgeous moustache shaved off. A humble gaunt soldier of short stature was in the crowd of soldiers instead of Napoleon. Some kind girl gave him a red tulip. M-r Felix Brandeveaux was so touched that he smelled that beautiful but completely odorless flower, and sang:

"Tis the last cause to battle…"

The living lighted crowded Paris surrounded by the great desert that was just at its outskirts was rejoicing, singing and dreaming of bright future — newly toiled fields and rebuilt factories, all night long. Parisians did not want to sleep. Sleep was dreadful. Sleep was like death and wilderness.

The chairman of "SORE" sat at the former prime minister's office and drew a plan of Europe's reconstruction. Tall and upright he bent over the numbers as if praying to his goddess — Justice. Around 8 AM he has succumbed to sleep sitting in his armchair after many sleepless nights. He was still smiling in his sleep.

At 8:15 in the morning m–r Felix Brandeveaux's most loyal troops began the cleansing operation to rid Paris of the most dangerous elements. They had the city's plan with underlined addresses, the lists of the leaders and poison gas guns equipped with silencers. By 10 in the morning the entire center of Paris was in the hands of legitimate government as well as Passy, Hauteville and Champs–Elysees.

Victor Brandeveaux was woken up by the guard's yell:

— We are trapped!

Victor Brandeveaux quickly got an abbot's cassock out of his trunk, put it on, folded his arms piously and calmly passed by the block posts of the army that had entered the city in such a treacherous way mumbling "Ave Maria." An hour later he was issuing orders at the regional council of Gobelins factory:

— Artillery fire at Champs-Elysees, Bomber pilots. Outflanking maneuver toward Montparnasse. Gases! Quickly!

Poor Parisians who had not slept all night hoped for some rest in the morning. But their hopes were dashed. They ran down the streets crying. Death was falling down from the skies. There was only one way out: underground, to the metro!

Cannons roared. Airplanes circled in the air like birds of prey. Buildings were collapsing. But all Paris was already underground. The soldiers of m-r Felix Brandeveaux followed civilians hiding from the artillery barrages. The pilots kept hunting down defenders of "SORE," and revolutionaries also hid in underground holes.

Thousands of people were fighting each other in the narrow platforms. There were no more innovations of the seven departments of defense ministry. People strangled each other like their ancestors did in pristine forests, like savages did in the great wilderness — enemies, friends, women, old people even rare children.

Power stations were long dead. It was completely dark underground. People ran down the long black tunnels, down the sewer pipes over which Seine was flowing. Quiet battles raged on in the dark. The only weapons remaining were nails and teeth.

Pilots circling over Paris shot each other down by and by. Ruins were strewn with the remnants of crushed planes. Only one "Whale" fighter plane was still circling serenely over that madness. Jens Boot was in it.

"D. E. Trust Co." director was watching the death throes of beautiful Paris through his field binoculars. Once he saw that all the remaining people had hidden underground and that the city streets have emptied completely, he landed, took out a diving suit out of plane's cockpit and put it on hastily. He looked closely at the river under which the metro tunnels ran.

And people there were still crushing, strangling, gnawing each other. Victor Brandeveaux was running down a long tunnel. It was incredibly hot there. Thick soapy air was pressing on his head and reminded him the last night in Berlin, the hot innards of steel monster. And just like then his heart that was counting seconds loudly seemed to be an excellent chronometer. Victor Brandeveaux was feeling time acutely with all his essence, he was not thinking about imminent death. An entire so called "history" — from Pharaoh Pherunkhanun's last aphorisms to the terrible end of "SORE" seem like a single short day to him. Real time began where the cooling yolk of the sun was hanging, where the dwarves covered in red bristly hair were crawling among the cacti, kangaroo-rats and spiders. They had earthworm's bodies. They drank thick blood and cried "choo-choo!." He knew now who they were. And his chronometer of the heart was beating precisely apprehending those terrible descendants. Suddenly somebody's stripped hot hand grabbed Victor Brandeveaux's throat.

— This is the grandson, — he whispered and turned on his pocket flashlight. Dim light exposed teeth as sharp as rat's incisors that bit Victor Brandeveaux's neck.

But that was no grandson, but just his own uncle, the genius of prime minister of Great France m-r Felix Brandeveaux. He screamed going completely mad:

— Choo-choo!

Piercing Victor's neck he tried to suck his thick heavy blood.

The rescue came unexpectedly, if it may be called a rescue: both were swallowed by cool streaming water.

The were no more defenders of m-r Felix Brandeveaux, nor the adherents of "SORE" in the black long tunnels, just waters of a quiet small river Seine that had decided the outcome of the underground battle for Europe's destiny.

Up on the ground at the river bank near the ruins of Notre Dame Jens Boot changed his attire. At 4:40 PM he left for foreign and faraway America that never had either Lucie or love, or long black tunnels in his "Whale" fighter plane leaving his diving suit and an excellent drill to dead Europe.

30
Emigration, Dividends, Nostalgia

On the Holy week of 1940 American Mormons led by Mr. Twyweight prayed for sinful and rightfully punished by God Europe.

In the spring of 1940 storks haven't left Egypt. In all other respects spring of 1940 was not much different than it was in previous years in the remaining four parts of the world. It was normal spring, a bit too rainy in America.

Europeans that have crossed the Atlantic were subjected to thorough disinfection. They spend spring in a quarantine. But they didn't murmur. They kissed that ground that smelled of coal and crude, the rough skin of America. They enjoyed the bloody stench of Chicago, the sooty air of Pittsburgh, the screeching machines, black sweat, Yankees' yelling and their own slave labor at the oil refineries in Ohio or at the steel mills of Mr. Jabbs. They munched corn affectionately, since US president issued an executive order that has limited civil rights of European immigrants, in particular — they were fed cornmeal instead of bread, which was nutritious enough for those low-bred creatures. However, cornmeal was better than poison gas, centrifuges and ciquita, and the coal mine shafts were cozier than black tunnels of former capital of France. Emigrants ate cornmeal and sang the hymnal of gratitude consisting of a single world: "Merci! Merci! M-e-r-r-c-i!"

Some Europeans have crossed Mediterranean. Arabs famous for their hospitality settled them in their houses and served them excellent coffee and rosy sorbet. Europeans stole their silver spoons, infected their women with venereal diseases and even demanded that the natives must create a special parliament for them and carry them on their shoulders. The Arabs then threw them out of their homes having prayed to Allah before doing that. The refugees have moved to the desert. They settled in some of the oases. Hot sand burned their noses. Eyes were sore from exposure to burning sun. There were no protective goggles, nor any lemonade. But Europeans still kissed that hot sand — the fierce face of bronze Africa. The lion's roar seemed like choy music to them after the cannons of m-r Felix Brandeveaux. Sandstorms were nothing compared to poison gas attacks. Europeans blessed their new fatherland reminiscing Europe.

In the Ural Mountains, where the heels of lazy beauty rested, still stood a pole with inscription:

$$\text{Europe} \leftarrow \dots \rightarrow \text{Asia}$$

European survivors came to it and hugged it superstitiously like some sort of talisman. Vast desert was behind and blessed realm laid ahead — Russia, Asia, peace.

Refugees were registered at Peoples' Commissariat of Labor where they were assigned a job. Russia was experiencing an industrial boom and had high demand for work force: Europeans worked mostly near lake Baikal at the centers of heavy industry. In Bratsk alone two hundred thousand immigrants were registered and occupied in metallurgy. Some have reached Sakhalin and worked at the coal mines there. Siberia had plenty of everything: snow, gold, bread and justice. Refugees did not reminisce of warm Crimean nights and cherry orchards of the Ukraine. Refugees worked, studied the basics of Marxism and blessed world proletariat not daring to bless abolished God. They brought new adage to Siberia: "He who sang "International" made it all the way to Ural." They were happy.

Some Europeans have even reached far, faraway Australia and commenced tending flocks of fat tail sheep immediately with blissful smiles. It seems like those were former Sorbonne professors.

The only European who suffered awful paroxysms of nostalgia was located at the 32nd floor of a midsize high–rise building. It was "D. E. Trust Co" director, who had finally carried out his grandiose plan.

After arriving to his New York bureau by airplane on July 4, Jens Boot immediately took out his portable typewriter and typed letters to Messrs. Jabbs, Hardyle and Twyweight.

"D. E. Trust Co." New York
July 4, 1940. #16814

Dear Sir,

Due to the fulfillment of the tasks of "D. E. Trust Co." you are invited to liquidation meeting that will take part on July 11 of this year at the Trust company's office.

Yours sincerely,

Jens Boot, executive director.

(Jens Boot was absolutely correct speaking of the Trust company's fulfilled tasks since fourteen bridges across the Detroit–river were already constructed and there was no more need for "Engineering Trust Co. of Detroit").

At the meeting the board members were again discussing the different brands of cigars. However, businesslike Mr. Twyweight had mentioned matter–of–factly:

— We ought to say something about the trust company. I don't think we have to share the dividends: the sense of justice carried out cannot be measured by any sums of money. The posterity that is bred in accordance with my eugenic treatises will be forever grateful.

— You are quite right, — Mr. Jabbs seconded. — A razor must cost four dollars. It is immoral to sell it for twenty cents! Mankind will thank us.

As for Mr. Hardyle, he just smiled victoriously. His smile can be explained by three circumstances:

1. He now became the king of oil instead of being an heir apparent before.

2. He has attained world renown after publishing his "Diary"

3. Having married for the second time he has completed all the procedures successfully.

Mr. Hardyle said still smiling victoriously:

— The work of the trust company allowed me do discover Central European wilderness. I am quite satisfied with my contribution. All lawful husbands of all times and nations will be forever grateful to me. As for my second spouse Mrs. Mary, she is already grateful.

Jens Boot listened to deliberations of the esteemed Americans with pleasant smile: he looked at the window at the same time — the beautiful Phoenician was waiting for him far, far-away in the East.

— We must thank out dear director, — Mr. Twyweight suggested. — I reward him with a million dollars, a luxury villa at the Pacific coast and a can of "Twyweight's" best meat filet in the world.

— I reward him with a mansion in New York City, a park in California, a salon train, five airplanes, twenty automobiles and the best razor in the world, — Mr. Jabbs replied.

Mr. Hardyle's present was the most original one:

— The day before yesterday I have paid off the state debt of Venezuela and therefore acquired that not very big but very nice country. I present it to you, my dear Mr. Boot. It has plenty of first-class oil and very nice accommodating women. Besides, you can issue their postal stamps with your portrait.

— I beg your pardon I am so touched by your kind words that I need to go out to get some fresh air. Oh, I am impressed so much!

Saying that director of the liquidated trust company took an elevator to the roof, where the excellent airplane "Whale" was waiting for him.

No, he did not need Venezuela with postal stamps, neither the salon train, nor the dollars. He could not live parted from his love. Faithful lover looked eastward day and night.

Twelve years turned out to be long enough time to extinguish the part of the world where more than three hundred and fifty million people used to live. But those years could not extinguish love in Jens Boot's heart. We would have crossed out the subtitle of our book "The history of European demise" and replace it with "The history of unextinguishable love" lest we demeaned it in the eyes of some esteemed scientists.

"There is morning there now, — Jens Boot thought while getting inside the plane's cockpit. She is rubbing her eyes. She is waiting for me. There is a red forelock of dawn on her forehead."

An that was true: far in the east Europe was basking in the morning sun surrounded by the seas: southern ones teeming with octopi and strange sea shells and northern ones teeming with silver herring.

Flying in the dusk over smoky New York City Jens Boot cried:

— To you!.. To you at once!.. Phoenician, I am yours!...

Three billionaires waited in vain for him to come back.

31
Zeus and Europe

Jens Boot did not look at the dashboard or the map. He smelled the air like a wild animal and that ancient sense alone led the modern fighter plane "Whale" At long last he landed somewhere at the very heart of Europe.

The clear days of early fall were there. Light wind was blowing golden maple, ash and alder leaves. Jens Boot had cut himself a walking staff and walked across the golden roadless plain. He walked for a long time. Red feverish land opened its lips thirstily. Brief rain showers quenched its thirst. At nights the skies were on fire and resounding lightning bolts hit the forests. Elderberry bushes have spread over half of Europe and its red berries shone with grief and passion. He heard buzzard's cackling during the day and owls' hooting at night. St. John's wort was blooming with its yellow flowers, agile ground beetles squeaked their wing-cases. Europe was still alive, and Jens Boot had rejoiced tremendously witnessing it.

He recognized his old familiars. Feral pigs that were now streamlined and agile like wild boars crossed his way. Crazy eyes of old cranks — the cats were seen in the trees. Chicken soared easily and clucked joyfully in the air. The most ancient insect of Europe cockroach left the smoky kitchens and proudly showed his long antennae on the oak bark.

Free and ignorant animals looked bewildered at their strange biped companion. But no animal did any harm to Jens Boot. Once he saw a she-wolf with a joyful litter of pups in the ruins of some gothic building that used to be a courthouse.

That she-wolf looked at a lonely man with motherly tenderness and licked his foul-smelling cheeks with her dry warm tongue.

Jens Boot walked for a long time, for days, weeks, perhaps even months. His face was overgrown with thick magnificent beard. He took off his suit that had been torn over the bushes and had just a long white shirt still on that looked like ancient togue. Tall staff cut out of an old ash served him as a support. The tree branches parted and rustled their leaves when he passed by. Jens Boot knew that that was Europe talking to him. How could the beautiful Phoenician not recognize her first and only lover — great Zeus in that old man possessed by forbidden passion?

And so, the evening came when Jens Boot finally stopped being exhausted. He was among the ruins of some city. A big brown bear sat at the doors of former stock exchange looking afar with his green-blue eyes and thoroughly licking his hardworking paws. Jens Boot staggered to it and gave it a meager leaf of grass half-frozen by the night frost. The bear took it amiably and put it down on a mossy stone. Jens Boot realized then that the solemn hour has come.

A broken rusty sign was on the ground next to him. Shuddering with emotion Jens Boot read:

EUROPE.

It was probably the name of some insurance agency or hotel. But Jens Boot knew only one thing: that was the name of his love. He ran and yelled:

— Europe! Europe!

There was wild red sunset over him. The great desert was all around him.

The last man was calling the name of proud Phoenician.

Jens Boot thrashed around full of passion and death, thrashed like a bull, thrashed like God. Then he fell. Warm lips were pressed to the ground that smelled of shamrock and wormwood. The last kiss! And Europe has recalled the wild charge and sweaty hairy neck of the bull that had abducted her, she recognized her lover. She has answered a kiss with a kiss.

And an hour later a white harrier was circling over dead Jens Boot and a sudden gust of the wind was playing with his grey beard.

Night has fallen. Phoenician princess dreamed peacefully surrounded by the seas in the south and in the north.

Thus, the last man of Europe Jens Boot had died.

Mormons of the world, let us pray for the sinful soul of great adventurer! Girls of the remaining four parts of the world, do remember that untamable lover in your tender dreams!

Berlin, February—March, 1923.

About the translator

ALEXANDER PINSKY was born in Moscow in 1955. He studied medicine at 2nd Moscow Medical Institute (now Russian State Medical University) in 1973–79, worked as a pediatrician in Moscow Emergency Medical Service till 1985, then went through two years of subspecialty training in pediatric anesthesiology and intensive care in 1985–87, then worked at Pediatric ICU till 1989.

He emigrated USSR and moved to the USA in 1989.

After passing Medical Board exams in January, 1991 he worked as a resident physican in New Jersey (Monmouth Medica Center), New York (Beth Israel Medical Center) and New Hampshire (Dartmouth-Hitchcock Medical Center). After graduating the residency program practiced pediatrics in Connecticut, New York and Pennsylvania. Alexander retired in 2025.

Translating literature is his main hobby. His first major translation into Russian of the the novel "Any Old Iron" by Anthony Burgess was published in Moscow in 2004 in the "Foreign Literature" Magazine, a year later was published as a separate volume by "Illuminator" publishing house in Moscow. The translation of the novel "The Patriots" by Sana Krasikov (together with Timothy Friedman) was published by M•Graphics in 2020.

This book is his first major translation from Russian into English.

www.ingramcontent.com/pod-product-compliance
Lightning Source LLC
Chambersburg PA
CBHW050404030726
47503CB00006B/2010